THE SPLENDID OUTCAST

Beryl Markham's
African Stories

Compiled and Introduced by Mary S. Lovell

LIBRARY
VT TECHNICAL COLLEGE
RANDOLPH CTR VT 05061

A LAUREL TRADE PAPERBACK

Published by
Dell Publishing
a division of
The Bantam Doubleday Dell
Publishing Group, Inc.
666 Fifth Avenue
New York, New York 10103

Copyright © 1987 by the Beryl Markham Estate
Introduction and Notes copyright © 1987 by Mary S. Lovell

All rights reserved. No part of this book may be reproduced or
transmitted in any form or by any means, electronic or mechanical,
including photocopying, recording, or by any information storage
and retrieval system, without the written permission of the Publisher, except where permitted by law.
For information address: North Point Press, San Francisco,
California.

The trademark Laurel ® is registered in the U.S. Patent and Trademark Office.

ISBN: 0-440-50030-3

Reprinted by arrangement with North Point Press

Printed in the United States of America

Published simultaneously in Canada

October 1988

BOMC offers recordings and compact discs, cassettes
and records. For information and catalog write to
BOMR, Camp Hill, PA 17012.

Beryl Markham

THE SPLENDID OUTCAST

"MARKHAM'S TALE-TELLING IS LYRICAL, SCENE-SETTING STUFF, THE STUFF THAT DELIGHTFUL STORIES ARE MADE OF . . . Every story is a pleasure to read, satisfying and delightful. They're warm bedtime reading, not only for adults, but for children as well." —*The Houston Post*

"ONE IS CONSTANTLY . . . REMINDED OF HEMINGWAY . . . both in style and quality of writing (spare, restrained, rugged) and in substance (e.g. courage, Africa, adventure)." —*St. Petersburg Press*

"A WELCOME ADDITION TO MARKHAM'S SLIM YET POTENT LITERARY OUTPUT. The stories mirror Markham's adventures in aviation, horse racing, and her African upbringing." —*Seattle Times/Post-Intelligencer*

"EFFECTIVE AND ENJOYABLE. . . . Admirers of *West with the Night*, hungry for more of Beryl Markham's unique writing, should find these stories a satisfying appetizer." —*St. Louis Post-Dispatch*

"THE DREAMY, ETHEREAL VOICE OF *WEST WITH THE NIGHT* THAT EVOKED HIGH PRAISE FROM CRITICS . . . tells some of the eight African stories in *The Splendid Outcast*, a few of which could seemlessly have been inserted into the memoir, they are in keeping with its tone." —*USA Today*

"SPLENDID . . . [THE STORIES] ARE OLD-FASHIONED IN A WAY THAT SHOULD NEVER GO OUT OF STYLE. They have linear plots and vivid descriptions, with more incident than introspection, more adventure than epiphany. They are at home in airfields or racetracks or a Masai village. They create a desire for resolution and, not always predictably, satisfy it." —*Greensboro News & Record*

"[THE STORIES] HAVE AN ABSOLUTE SURENESS OF SUBJECT MATTER, MAINLY HORSES AND AFRICAN FRONTIER LIFE, and the poignant lyricism of Markham's memoir."
—*The Plain Dealer* (Cleveland)

"EIGHT STORIES . . . RESCUED FROM THE COBWEBS OF TIME. . . . The reader who has fallen in love with Markham's prose in *West with the Night* will read them all." —*The Virginian-Pilot and Ledger-Star*

"SUSPENSEFUL, WELL SHAPED, and similar in tone to the wonderful stories from *West with the Night*." —*The Philadelphia Inquirer*

"VIVID WITH DETAILS OF AFRICAN CUSTOM AND LANDSCAPE gleaned from the author's early life in Kenya."
—*Publishers Weekly*

For Beryl's granddaughters
Fleur and Valery
In memory of their father
Gervase Markham

Contents

Introduction

Beryl Markham had an extraordinary life. Her parentage and her birthplace ought to have guaranteed her a life within the comfortable constraints of Edwardian "county" society, a life in which she would have received a formal education of English literature, French grammar, painting, and needlework taught by governesses. Dressed in restricting crinoline and pantaloons, Beryl might have sat gazing dreamily out of schoolroom windows onto the Leicestershire countryside, or played with dolls on the shaved green lawns under the cedars of her childhood home, occasionally hearing the slow clop, clop of a passing horse beyond the confining hedges. Later she would have been taught to ride, and, inevitably, to ride to hounds, for her home in Ashwell was at the heart of the finest fox hunting country in England and her parents were both keen fox hunters. Perhaps, later still, she would have joined the eager throngs of debutantes, primped for her first ball, and eventually married some suitable neighboring landowner. Though by any flight of fancy it is difficult to imagine Beryl being content to spend her days in a silk-lined drawing room dispensing tea and gossip.

But in 1903 her father decided to emigrate to the burgeoning Protectorate of British East Africa, now Kenya. Beryl was only three years old when she was taken out to join him on an isolated pioneer homestead where the emphasis in education was on survival. Within eighteen months her parents had separated and her mother returned to England taking the eldest child, Richard, with her. Beryl remained on the farm at Njoro with her father and thus began a unique upbringing almost devoid of convention or restriction, which she called "a world without walls."

Beryl's father was fully occupied with the business of establishing his farm, so the child was left in the daily care of African workers. As naturally as breathing she learned the customs and languages of the numerous tribespeople who squatted on the farm: Nandi, Kipsigis, Luo, Kikuyu, even the occasional Masai herdsman. With these friends as mentors she ran barefoot, and often half naked, through primeval forests. She learned to hunt and track with native cunning, and to kill wild animals armed only with a spear. She became part of Africa and Africa became part of her.

Sometimes Beryl joined her father on his rounds of the farm, riding her pony, an Arab stallion named Wee MacGregor. As time went by she graduated to exercising the imported English thoroughbred racehorses that her father trained as a sideline to his farming interests. Before she was in her teens she was riding and handling horses that were too "difficult" for the African syces [grooms]. Her riding ability and knowledge of horses had become a legend in Kenya even before she trained the winner of the St. Leger.

It was a hard life and the presence of a thousand African migrant workers did not provide a leisurely existence for Beryl and her father. The days were long and arduous and the foes of the pioneer settler were many. Marauding lions and leopards killed the stock—the stock that had survived tick fever or other numerous endemic ailments. Other wild animals trampled or grazed upon crops. The vagaries of climate—too much sun and no rain, and then suddenly too much rain—had to be contended with while the farm was literally hacked out of the Mau forest.

Sometimes in the long dark evenings after the rows of thoroughbred horses had been bedded down, Beryl would sit before the blazing cedarwood fire and her father would read aloud from the Greek classics by the light of a hurricane lamp. Once she had learned to read, she read voraciously from any book that came her way, and later her father appointed governesses—a chain of them—all heartily disliked. Two male tutors were tolerated until the First World War called both into service, when the rebellious Beryl was sent away to school in Nairobi.

She was always a difficult pupil because she resented discipline, and after three years she was expelled for inciting fellow pupils to revolt. She returned happily to Njoro and became "head lad" in her father's racing stable. Two weeks before her seventeenth birthday, a tall, patrician, and extremely beautiful young woman, Beryl was married to a neighboring farmer who was twice her age. Shortly after her marriage, her father went bankrupt and left the country, so at the age of eighteen she obtained a trainer's license, took over the training of a handful of horses and immediately produced winners. When her marriage disintegrated she moved into a grass-thatched hut, continued training, and was only twenty-three years old when she trained the winner of the Kenya St. Leger. More success followed, as did a second brief marriage to a wealthy aristocrat. But the marriage failed when she became emotionally entangled with an English prince, and she threw her career over without a backward glance when she became interested in the new sport of flying.

Beryl did not see flying as a sport, however. She saw it as a new and exciting way to earn a living. She obtained her pilot's license and quickly built up her flying hours, including a solo six-thousand-mile flight to England when she had only just over a hundred hours in her logbook. Then she went on to gain her commercial pilot's license—the first awarded to any woman in East Africa. In her flimsy, fabric-covered biplane she hired herself out as a big-game spotter to safari parties. Using cleared areas of scrub as temporary landing strips, she joined the hunters and flew each day looking for herds of elephant, especially the big "tuskers" sought by the trophy hunters. When the safari season ended, she ferried passengers to isolated "up-country" farms, carried the air mails to gold miners in Tanganyika, turned her two-seater into a flying ambulance, and occasionally worked as a relief pilot for a newly established airline. The solo flying she did across the bush was highly dangerous, given the technical restrictions of aircraft at that time and the wilderness over which she flew. She had no radio, and a forced landing—even assuming she survived it without injury—could have meant slow death from starvation or thirst, not to mention attack by wild animals. Her only concession to the dangers was to carry a phial of morphine in the pocket of her immaculate white flying suit, and a revolver.

In 1936 Beryl was the first woman to fly the Atlantic from east to west—the first person of either sex to fly from England to North America—and she became an international celebrity. There was a handful of famous aviators at the time represented in the United States by Charles Lindbergh, Amelia Earhart, and Wiley Post, and in England by Amy Johnson, Jim

Mollison, and Jean Batten, all had written their stories (or, in some cases, had them ghostwritten). It was therefore inevitable that Beryl should be asked to write about her achievement, but the book that resulted, *West with the Night*, was a revelation. Far from being a stereotyped version of how she learned to fly, followed by the Atlantic crossing, her memoir drew upon her childhood and equine experiences, as well as her aeronautical exploits, and was written in a style that earned praise from literary critics. But after a brief period of success during which the book reached number one on the *New York Times* bestseller list, it faded into obscurity, a forgotten victim of the Second World War.

When, forty years later, her beautifully phrased book was rediscovered and republished, doubt was thrown upon Beryl's ability to have written it. Friends of Beryl's third husband, the writer Raoul Schumacher, claimed it was he who had written Beryl's work. "She was nearly illiterate!" said some of her detractors, while others asked why—since she was so able—were there no other works? This collection of Beryl's short stories, discovered during research for her authorized biography, provide some answers.

After researching Beryl's fascinating career, meeting her, and discovering her range of talent, I find it incredible that anyone who knew her well could doubt her ability to write. Who else could have told the story of her childhood and other experiences with such depth and perception? No ghostwriter could have extracted the level of detail and produced it so sensitively.

The supposition that Beryl was illiterate is pure nonsense. She had an education all right, though it was not always formal in its structure. It was sufficiently good to enable her to pass her commercial pilot's examinations, including the difficult Navigation Theory paper. Her pilot's logbook reveals a firm, educated hand, and her surviving letters convey a light sense of humor and a neat phraseology. Her learning process was an uncoordinated mixture of the practical and the aesthetic, helped along on occasions by her well-educated father, and later still by the scholarly Denys Finch Hatton, who encouraged Beryl to educate herself.

Beryl herself always maintained that she was the sole author of her book. Equally, she claimed that it was her old friend, the French writer/aviator Antoine de Saint-Exupéry, who helped her to start writing her memoir (perhaps accounting for its poetic nature), and she never denied that Raoul helped her with editorial advice and support. There are some surviving pages of manuscript that bear Raoul Schumacher's handwritten edits, and Beryl herself acknowledged his "help and encouragement" in a foreword. But she wrote the major part of her memoir in the Bahamas and Raoul never visited her there.

Beryl herself seemed totally unconcerned about the theory that she had not written the book. When I discussed the subject with her she dismissed it, "Oh that old thing again!" Asked how she answered her detractors, she shrugged and said, "I don't bother. . . ."

Writing was only incidental to Beryl, to be cast off when she moved on to the next phase of her life. After her marriage to Raoul Schumacher foundered in 1948 she returned to Africa and embarked upon a second brilliant career training racehorses. Her long life was filled with adventure and achievement. Her other great successes—the horse training and the flying—were public, often in the glare of media coverage. But writing cannot be done in public. It is essentially a lonely profession and therefore it was easy for Beryl's detractors to cast doubt on her authorship.

My opinion is that Beryl—like many who have confined their writing to autobiography—found writing a chore. Though she called herself a writer during her American period and often made a show of retiring to her room "to work," she had difficulty in producing finished pieces of fiction. Nonetheless, during her American period Beryl published the stories contained in this anthology, some of which share the vivid classical quality that singles out *West with the Night* as a great piece of writing. The others are of less interest as literature than for their historical background, because there is much in them that enhances what is known about Beryl's life.

Beryl cooperated with me in the writing of her biography, but she died before I could tell her that I was compiling this anthology, which was to be a surprise for her eighty-fourth birthday. I can therefore only imagine what her reaction would have been. "Really? How funny! Sit down and have a drink. Now . . . what shall we talk about?" To the end she remained essentially modest about her achievements. When she spoke of them at all it was matter-of-factly and when asked to elaborate, a dismissive wave of her long slim hands was inevitably accompanied with a scornful, "But it's all so long ago, no one will be interested in that."

Beryl's literary works are few, and that is our loss. But now that her autobiography promises to rank among the classics of our time she surely deserves the full, unequivocal credit for her remarkable writing ability, in addition to the acclaim that she has already received for her other achievements.

MARY S. LOVELL
Salisbury, England
March 1987

PART ONE

Something I Remember

This story and the two that follow are almost autobiographical and form a welcome addition, in Beryl's own words, to her memoir. I use the word almost because in each case the facts have been slightly exaggerated to provide a dramatic climax to real events. It may well be that originally she had written about these episodes for her memoir. It is known that her husband Raoul advised her to cut that work down and revise the chronology, and perhaps the resultant discards provided the basis for these individual short stories, which were finished at a later date.

At the time Beryl wrote this story, she was living on an isolated New Mexico ranch where she "raised turkey poults and did a lot of riding." She told me that Raoul was sometimes away due to war service and she was often bored and lonely. Recalling and writing about her childhood helped to pass the long evenings.

Wee MacGregor was Beryl's first horse. Her father bought him when Beryl was about six years old, and it is typical of Beryl that her first horse was an Arab stallion, a type not normally known for docility. But Beryl's remarkable riding ability was obvious even as a tiny child—she describes Wee MacGregor as an obedient pony.

It is not known whether the fight between Wee MacGregor and Chaldean actually happened. Certainly there was a filly in Beryl's stable called

[First published in *Collier's, The National Weekly*, January 1944.]

Reve d'Or in 1922; it was her father's parting gift when he left Kenya for Peru. The incident described here is more likely to be the reflection of several fights between stallions, witnessed by Beryl at Green Hills—the Njoro farm where she grew up.

———————

When I think about it, it seems to me that in twenty-odd years of breeding and training racehorses, I ought to have encountered at least one with human qualities. I have read about such horses but I have never known one and I can't help feeling a little cheated. Whenever I have heard someone say, "Now there's a horse so intelligent he's almost human," I have had to admit to myself a little sadly that no horse I can bring to memory ever deserved that laudatory phrase. Of course, it may be that such a comparison is, to a horse, of doubtful virtue. That was certainly the case with Wee MacGregor.

Wee MacGregor maintained throughout his life a gentle contempt for both men and the works of men, and I am convinced that his willing response to their demands was born wholly of tolerance. He rarely ignored a word or resisted a hand; and it was not until he began his blood feud with Chaldean that anyone realized the intensity of the fire that burned in his heart.

Wee MacGregor was an Arab. His coat was chestnut, and his mane and tail were black, and he wore a white star on his forehead—jauntily and a little to one side, more or less as an impudent street urchin might wear his cap. He was an urchin, too, by the standards prevailing in our stables. He was perfectly built but very small, and though he was a stallion, he was not bought to breed, certainly not to race, but only to work at carrying myself or my father—and even, if need be, to draw a pony cart. I still remember the day he came.

Horses were always coming and going on our farm in Kenya. Some arrived for training, and others left for the races at Nairobi, Eldoret, Nakuru, or even Durban, more than two thousand miles away. Until the advent of Wee MacGregor, they were all thoroughbreds of course and, to the uninitiated, they must have looked alike, except for color. They were tall, tense horses of supreme arrogance and insolent beauty. They were pampered, they were groomed, they were cherished like the heirs to so many thrones.

They were, I am afraid, a snobbish clique, for when Wee MacGregor was led for the first time to his stall (in the lesser stable) he was greeted with silence. Not even a stallion raised his voice, and the brood mares in their spacious boxes scarcely stirred. There may have been other reasons for it, but the controlled dismay with which our thoroughbreds looked upon Wee MacGregor was, in effect, similar to the way a gathering of the socially illustrious might view the arrival in their midst of a laborer with calloused hands.

Nevertheless, in the days that followed, the little Arab worked hard and kept his peace; he toiled with patience and gave everyone to understand that he bore no grudge and that his was a placid soul. He was intelligent, he handled beautifully, he refused no effort asked of him, and it may have been that if Chaldean had not come to the farm, we would never have been disillusioned about Wee MacGregor's pacific nature. But Chaldean did come—and on a bad day, too.

We were clearing the trees from our farm—or rather we were fighting the great Mau forest, which, in its centuries of unhampered growth, had raised a rampart of trees so tall I used to think their branches brushed the sky. The trees were cedar, olive, yew, and bamboo, and often the cedars rose to heights of two hundred feet, blocking the sun.

Men said the forest could not be beaten, and this was true, but at least my father made it retreat. Under his command, a corps of Dutchmen with hundreds of oxen and an axe to every man assaulted the bulwark, day after day, and in time its outer walls began to fall.

On one such day, my father said to me, "Get Wee Mac-Gregor and take this note to Mostert. The rains are due, and I don't want the teams bogged in the forest."

Christiaan Mostert was our foreman and when, an hour later, he took my father's message from my hand and read it, he looked upward involuntarily, but he could not see the sky.

"Ja," he said, "I see nothing, but I think the baas is right. I smell rain, and the monkeys have lost their tongues."

He spat on his hands and shouted an order, but it was too late. Thunder swallowed his voice, and rain swallowed the forest. It was a typical equatorial storm—instantaneous, violent, and all-encompassing. It made the world black, then split the blackness with knives of light. It made the great trees creak and the bamboos moan. Forest hogs ran for cover, terrified parrots darted in green and scarlet arcs through the lightning, and the oxen plunged and strained in their traces.

It was not a new thing for Christiaan Mostert, or for any of his men, or for me. It was new for Wee MacGregor, and yet the little Arab took the whole monstrous nightmare in his stride. He neither reared nor even trembled, and as I rode him from ox team to ox team through the roaring forest aisles, his manner was one of dutiful resignation.

Even when a massive cedar, ripped by lightning, fell across a span of oxen and broke the backs of two, he did not wince; and when Christiaan Mostert put rifle bullets into the suffering beasts, Wee MacGregor only tilted his ears in mild curiosity, as if the insanity of his masters had begun to bore him.

For an hour he worked, disdainful even of the storm, lending his strength to a bogged wagon more than once, carrying me back and forth with Mostert's orders to his men; and when the storm ended as abruptly as it had begun, Wee MacGregor met Chaldean for the first time.

Chaldean had arrived that day from England. He stood, bristling arrogance, blanketed and angry-eyed in the broad space between our stables. My father was there, standing proudly beside him, and a dozen syces and farm boys, marveling at his beauty.

It was more than beauty. It was pride in heritage and consciousness of ability, for Chaldean's breeding and his record were clean as fire. He was a descendant of St. Simon, and a champion, and his colts were champions and he knew it.

He was black and smooth as a rifle barrel and as hard. The cast of his head was classic. He was deep-chested and clean-legged and the promise of a magnificent stride lay in his height and in the power of his quarters. He was to Wee MacGregor as a Doric column to a beam of wood, and he clothed his beauty in insolence.

Wee MacGregor felt it. Straight from his labors in the forest, still wet with the rain that mingled with his sweat, he raised his head and looked upon this pampered paragon—and trembled. He let a low sound escape his throat, and Chaldean heard it.

For a moment, the two horses—one a drudge and one a prince—regarded each other, and then Chaldean whirled on his tether and reared from the ground and screamed the shrill scream of an angered stallion. He rose higher, against my father's strength, and beat the air with his forelegs and screamed again. My father swore and jerked him down, and the syces ran forward to hold him.

Wee MacGregor plunged, but I held him back. He fought the bridle, but I turned him. It did not last long, but it was not finished. I knew then, as I rode to the stable, that the giant. thoroughbred and the little Arab had made their quarrel and what remained was only the settling of it.

Still under the pressure of regular work, you forget such things. If you have a stable of fifty horses, you have not time to concern yourself with the grudges and foibles of one or two. You remember certain rules and you follow them. The rule that two warring stallions must never meet is axiomatic—so self-evident that you take it for granted that they never will.

My days passed, and when on occasion I had to use Wee MacGregor again on some routine duty or other, it did not seem to me that anything about him had changed. He brooded a lot, the way some horses do, or appear to do, and often I would find him in his stall standing in the farthest corner, out of the light, staring at the wall and seeing nothing.

It is true that once or twice I noticed that the wooden latch on his door had been partly slipped back, but there again I thought nothing of it because many horses will, out of boredom, fondle a latch with their teeth or toy with a halter rope. I always shot the latch home and forgot about it.

When Reve d'Or came to the farm, Chaldean's ego began to assert itself to such an extent that at times he was almost beyond control. Reve d'Or was a whaler filly (that is to say, an Australian thoroughbred filly), a dark bay and beautiful in the eyes of horsemen, but I never knew why her daily passage down the areaway between Chaldean's stable and Wee MacGregor's should have brought their vendetta to the white heat that it did; there were dozens of other mares and fillies on the place.

It may have been that, in fact, she was wholly forgotten

by both of them once they had established a new reason for
their enmity, but however that was, her groom never led her
past the stables without drawing from the little Arab and the
haughty thoroughbred screams of mutual rage and hatred. It
ought to have been obvious to everybody that one day this
burning bitterness must bring a climax, but no one thought
about it.

It was not so long a time that Reve d'Or had a lovely foal,
and Chaldean (since he was of St. Simon strain) was, of course,
its sire. Horse breeders are not given to romanticism in their
work but rather to considerations of profit and loss, and a colt
by Chaldean out of Reve d'Or gave great expectations to my
father and to those horse-wise friends who frequented our
house.

It is a strange but a true thing that the appearance of a new
foal in a stable will always excite the stallions and even the
geldings to the most exorbitant antics. They will neigh and
scream and beat against their boxes in a kind of wild gaiety. If
they are in pasture, they will gallop its length time and again,
kicking their heels, drumming out the good word with swift
and sparkling hooves like tireless performers at a week-long
jubilee. No birthdays go unheralded. And yet, in the case of
Reve d'Or's foal, Wee MacGregor was a silent bystander.

This, I suppose, was due to his breeding. Arabs are not so
excitable as thoroughbreds, and Wee MacGregor was valued
all the more for his steady (if increasingly dour) character. He
had even got to the point where he no longer returned Chaldean's insults, but only stood and glared at his enemy from the
darkest depths of his stall. He worked hard while Chaldean
basked in the sun; he arrived home clotted with sweat while
Chaldean fretted under the ministrations of some diligent
syce; his feet were left unshod for labor while Chaldean's were

deftly plated for glory on the track. We forgot, but Wee MacGregor remembered these things. He hoarded the memories until his heart was full of them and would hold no more.

It is a hideous thing to watch two stallions fight. If you are on the back of one, it is terrifying.

For many months, not a morning had passed on which Wee MacGregor had not seen me mount Chaldean and ride him away to his exercise. For many months, I had forgotten the half-open latch on Wee MacGregor's door, I had forgotten that patience and practice make for perfection. Nowadays I can only believe that Wee MacGregor knew it from the first.

He caught us not far from the house. The path we always took wandered through a wattle grove that had a clearing in it. It was a big clearing surrounded by trees and shaded by their lacelike leaves and yellow blossoms. The earth underneath was red clay and hard. It was so hard that it gave a kind of ring to Wee MacGregor's hooves—a bold and forthright ring, for he used no cunning in his attack; he did not come from behind.

He came straight for his enemy, not cantering or rushing headlong, but lifting his firm little legs high and proudly, making taut the bow of his neck, flaunting his black tail like a battle plume. Nor were his ears laid back in anger. They were alert, anticipant, and eager—as if this, at last, were the joyful moment he had dreamed of all his quiet life.

I remember that the little scraps of sunlight fallen through the leaves lay on his chestnut coat and burnished it like armor; I remember that his eyes were bright. I remember, too, that Chaldean swung round with graceful majesty to face this puny David and his shining courage. I could feel Chaldean's muscles harden; I could feel his veins swell to rigid ropes beneath his skin. I could hear the first notes of his battle cry, deep and low in his throat, and I looked around me.

Through the trees I could see our house, but it was far. No one was near—not my father, not a syce, not a farmhand. I might have dismounted, but you do not abandon a valuable horse to his fury; you do not throw away the rules. You hang on—and tremble. I hung on. I trembled. The two stallions were alone in their anger and I was alone in my fear.

When Wee MacGregor charged, when Chaldean screamed his challenge, when blood spurted on my clothes and on my bare arms, and the cyclones of dust hid all but trenchant teeth and hooves like iron cudgels, my fear was frozen still—and I was a forgotten watcher.

I watched the little Arab's first lunge. He came in, head outstretched, swift as a sword, using only his teeth—flashing his teeth—hoping to cripple Chaldean's foreleg. He was fearless. He was quick, and in this quickness he was deadly.

Chaldean went to his knees, parrying the thrust and screaming his war cry with what seemed the volume of a thousand trembling trumpets. The vibrations of that cry ran through my body.

Chaldean went down. He struck his shoulder on a root, gashing the flesh, adding crimson to our vortex of whirling color, but he rose again with inspired fury. He reared high, while I clung to him, and he caught the Arab on the flank, striking both blood and pain as a smith strikes fire from steel.

I suppose I cried out. I suppose I flailed my whip and let the reins cut my tugging hands. I was alone and not yet fifteen, and it may even have been that I wept, but these are things I don't remember. I only remember the sudden realization of the terrible power, the destructive strength that can pour from the sinews of this most docile of animals, this nodding slave of men.

Wee MacGregor fought with so cold a determination that he made almost no sound. It was clear at once that he wanted not just to win but to kill. It was clear, too, that he felt that his anger compensated for his lack of size.

Chaldean towered above him. He had advantages and he used them. He reared until the Arab was beneath him, then plunged and sank his teeth into Wee MacGregor's neck and held fast and reared again and hurled his enemy from him into the dust and blood, and there was a moment of silence.

There was a moment of silence as the little Arab found his legs and stood sucking breath into his lungs. The wound on his neck was deep and it was scarlet, but it might have been no wound at all. He gave no sign of pain.

For a frantic instant, I tried to turn Chaldean, to drive him home, but he would not budge. He knew what was coming, and it came.

If Wee MacGregor had fought viciously before, he fought insanely now. He came in with eyes like burning coals, and I tried to beat him off, but for him, I was not there. For him, nothing existed save his anger and his enemy. Abandoning caution, he closed, and the impact almost threw me from the saddle.

Again Chaldean caught him by the neck and hurled him bleeding to the ground, and again he rose, staggering a little now, but not hesitating. His courage was like a shield that beat away the thought of fear. Three times he came on and three times he fell before Chaldean's strength and fury. But on the fourth try, he found his moment.

I do not know how it happened, but somehow in the maelstrom of screams and dust and thudding hooves, the little

Arab caught in his teeth a strip of the pressure bandage bound around Chaldean's foreleg. The bandage had come undone. It was like a net, and the Arab meant to make it one. He held it firmly in his teeth and pulled, and Chaldean was helpless. He pawed and plunged and tottered and swayed, fighting to free himself. There wa. panic in him—and I prepared to leap from his back at last. It seemed madness to hang on for, if he fell, I should fall with him—perhaps under him.

I beat Wee MacGregor with my whip, sparing no strength, lashing his head and his neck and his withers, but he was aware of nothing save the promise of triumph. His teeth clamped tight on the bandage, he threw the whole power of his body into the effort of downing his enemy.

Chaldean faltered. He was trapped, and the Arab knew it. I knew it. I put my hands on the pommel and made ready to throw myself clear, I could hear voices coming up the road, but now there was not time. It was too late.

I was raising myself from the saddle when the bandage broke in Wee MacGregor's teeth. The ripping of the cloth and Chaldean's lunge were simultaneous. So, almost, was my own cry and Wee MacGregor's single shriek of pain when Chaldean's teeth closed on the little Arab's foreleg, twisting it, breaking the bone as if it were a stalk of corn. Chaldean reared high and, for the last time, threw his challenger to earth.

The Arab lay almost still, but he was not dead, and Chaldean would not have it so. Not I, but his rage was master. Wee MacGregor tried once more to rise, but the bone of his leg was broken through. David was down, and Goliath moved forward to kill him, but he did not.

My father had come, and with him, his men. They had bound grass to sticks and made torches of them and now they beat Chaldean back with fire. They thrust the fire in his face and beat him back, step by step, and shouted at him, and I gathered the reins tight in my hands, which were bleeding now, and urged him home at last, down the dusty road, not bothering to hold my tears.

Most times you destroy a crippled horse, but Wee Mac-Gregor was made to live, though he never worked again. He was brought home on a rope stretcher and for weeks he stood in his stall supported by a sling until, in time, he walked once more, with halting steps.

Of course, he was never any trouble after that; he could not have been. He was pensioned, as faithful horses often are, and he never again slipped the latch of his stall—or at least not more than once.

One day, or rather at the end of one day, when the sun was almost gone and I rode Reve d'Or through the clearing in the wattle grove, we came upon the little Arab standing still as marble in what had been the arena of his great defeat. He was older then, and the fire had gone from his eye, and his chest-nut coat was dull in the horizontal light. But there he stood, looking not at Reve d'Or and not at me, but at the earth, and we passed him by. He did not whinny or make any sound or lift his head. He only stood there like a man with a dream.

But of course that was only the way it seemed to me. Horses are not like humans—at least no horse that I have ever known—and I suspect that he had come there only to catch the last warmth of the sun. I don't know, and so I can't be sure. It is all just something I remember.

The Captain and His Horse

*"The Captain and His Horse" was the first short story written by Beryl
while she was living in New York in 1943. It is based on a true incident—
the group of men and horses did visit the Njoro farm during the First World
War. When I interviewed Beryl in 1986 I had not seen this story, but she
had a page of draft manuscript for it and we discussed that. She recalled
the horse rather than the men, though she did remember playing cricket and
learning how to fire a revolver.*

*The name she gave to he horse in the story was poetic license. Beryl
thought the horse's name was "something funny like Jimmy . . . I can't remember exactly," she said. But there was a horse called the Baron in Beryl's
life. He was one of her first racehorses when she started training and was
part-owned by her great friend and lover, Tom Campbell Black.*

*The incident in this story probably happened in early 1915, for later
that year Beryl was sent away to school in Nairobi. In 1917 when she was
expelled for trying to incite a rebellion, she returned to Njoro to become
"head lad" at her father's racing stable, and then she was clearly older than
the girl portrayed here.*

*After the story was first published, Beryl's editor at Houghton Mifflin
wrote to the South African writer Stuart Cloete, a mutual friend, asking*

[First published in *Ladies' Home Journal*, August 1943.]

him if he had seen Beryl's "magnificent horse story" in a weekly magazine.
Cloete's reply reveals his exasperated amusement:

> *Yes I have read Beryl's magnificent horse story, and you will find my*
> *equally magnificent horse story in a forthcoming Collier's ["Crusader," first*
> *published in* Collier's, The National Weekly, 1943]. *I wrote mine*
> *some time before Beryl wrote hers and read it to her when she was in New*
> *York.*

Honi soit qui mal y pense . . .

The world is full of perfectly well-meaning people who are sentimental about the horse. They believe that God in His wisdom charged the horse tribe with two duties; the first being to serve man generally, and the second being to eat lump sugar from the palms of kindly strangers. For centuries the horse has fulfilled these obligations with little complaint, and as a result his reputation has become static, like that of a benevolent mountain, or of an ancient book whose sterling qualities most people accept without either reservation or investigation. The horse is "kind," the horse is "noble." His virtues are so emphasized that his character is lost.

The personalities of many horses have remained in my mind from early East African days. Horses peopled my life then and, in a measure, they still people my memory. Names like these—Cambrian, the Baron, Wee MacGregor—are to me bright threads in a tapestry of remembrance hardly tarnished after all these years.

Now there is war, and it is hard to say a thing or think a thing into which that small but most tyrannical of words does not insert itself. I suppose it is because of this that the name of the Baron comes most often to me—because of this and, of course, because, among other things, the Baron was himself a warrior. There was a war, too, when I was a girl of thirteen living on what was euphemistically called a Kenya farm, but which was in fact a handful of cedar huts crouching on alien earth and embraced by wilderness. That was the old war, the nearly forgotten war, but it had the elements of all wars: it bred sorrow and darkness, it bred hope, and it threw strong lights on the souls of men, so that you could see, sometimes, courage that you never knew was there.

Like all wars—like this one—it produced strange things. It brought people together who had never before had a common cause or a common word. One day it brought to my father's farm at Njoro a small company of sick and tired men—mounted on horses that were tired, too—who had the scars of bullets in their flesh.

It goes without saying that the men were cast of heroic stuff. I remember them. A man who has fought for six months in blinding desert heat and stinging desert cold and lives only to fight again has no respect for the word "heroic." It is a dead word, a verbal medal too nebulous to conceal even the smallest wound. Still, you can utter it—you can write it for what it is worth.

But these men came on horses. Each man rode a horse, each was carried to the restful safety of our farm not by an animal, but by his companion, by his battle friend.

"Who are they?" I asked my father.

He is a tall man, my father, a lean man, and he husbands his words. It is a kind of frugality, a hatred of waste, I think. Through all his garnered store of years, he has regarded wasted emotion as if it were strength lavished on futile things. "Save strength for work," he used to say, "and tears for sorrow, and space it all with laughter."

We stood that morning on the little porch of our mud-and-daub house, and I asked my father who these men were with torn clothes and bearded faces and harsh guns in such a gentle land. It is true that leopards came at night and that there were lions to be met with on the plains and in the valleys not far away. But we had learned to live with these and other beasts—or at least they had learned to live with us—and it seems to me now that it was a land gentle beyond all others.

"They are soldiers of the British army," my father said, "and they are called Wilson's Scouts. It is very simple. They have never seen you before, but they have been fighting for your right to grow up, and now they have come here to rest. Be kind to them—and above all, see to it that their horses want nothing. In their way, they are soldiers, too."

"I see," I said. But I was a child and I saw very little. In the days that followed, the tired men grew strong again and most of their wounds healed, and they would talk in the evening as they sat around our broad table. The men would sit under hurricane lamps whose flames danced when a joke was made, or grew steady again when there was silence. Sometimes the flames would falter, and I could stand in the room for long minutes nursing a failing lamp and hearing what there was to hear.

I heard of a German, General von Lettow-Vorbeck, who, with his Prussian-officered troops based in German East Africa, was striking north to take our country. It seemed that these troops were well-enough trained, that they responded to orders without question, like marionettes responding to strings. But they were lost men; they were fighting British settlers, they were trying to throw Englishmen out of their homes—an undertaking in which I sensed, even then, the elements of flamboyant ambition, and not a small measure of indiscretion.

They were well-enough trained, these Germans, but, among

other things, they had Wilson's Scouts to consider; hard-riding volunteer colonials whose minds were unhampered with military knowledge, but whose hearts were bitter and strong—and free. No, it seemed to me, as I listened to them, that the enemy they fought was close to his grave. And as things developed, he was, when I met the Baron, already anticipating its depth.

There was a captain in our small group of cavalrymen, and he would sometimes talk about the Baron—short snatches of talk of the kind that indicated that everybody everywhere must, of course, have heard of him. The captain would say things like this. He would say, "It looked difficult to me. There was a *donga* six feet across and deep with wait-a-bit thorns, and three of the enemy on the other side, but the Baron wasn't worried and so I couldn't be. We cleaned them out after a little skirmish—though the Baron caught one in the shoulder. He holds it still." And the other men would shake their heads and drink their drinks, which I knew was just a quiet way of paying tribute to the Baron.

He was the pride of the regiment, of course, but when I first saw him in the stable my father had given him near our thoroughbreds, I was disappointed. I couldn't have helped that; I was used to sensitive, symmetrical, highly strung horses, clean-bred and jealous of their breeding.

But the Baron was not like this. He was crude to look at. Surrounded by the aristocrats of his species, the Baron seemed a common animal, plebeian. It was almost as if he had been named derisively. At our first meeting he stood motionless and thoughtful—a dark brown gelding with a boxlike head. There was thick hair around his pasterns and fetlock joints, and he wore his rough coat indifferently, the way a man without vanity, used to war, will wear his tattered tunic.

It is a strange thing to say of a horse, but when I went into the Baron's stable I felt at once both at ease and a little inferior. I think it was his eyes more than anything—they were dark, larger than the eyes of most horses, and they showed no white. It wasn't a matter of their being kind eyes—they were eyes that had seen many things, understanding most of them and fearing none. They held no fire, but they were alive with a glow of wisdom, neither quiet nor fiercely burning. You could see in his eyes that his soul had struck a balance.

He turned to me, not wanting to smell my hair or to beg for food, but only to present himself. His breathing was smooth and unhurried, his manner that of an old friend, and I stroked his thick hard neck that was like a stallion's, because I could think of nothing else to do. And then I left quietly, though there was no need for silence, and walked through one of our pastures and beyond the farm into the edge of the Mau forest, where, if you were a child, it was easier to think.

I thought for a long time, concluding nothing, answering nothing, because there was nothing I could answer.

The war, the wounded men, the big thoughts, the broad purposes—all were still questions to me, beyond my answering. Yet I could not help but think that the dark brown gelding standing there in his stable was superior, at least to me, because he made it evident that he had no questions and needed no answers. He was, in his way, as my father had said, a soldier, too.

It is easy enough to say such a thing, but as one day nudged another through that particular little corridor of time the Baron proved himself a soldier—and it seems to me now, something more.

I don't think I ever learned the full name of the young captain who owned him, but that was not my fault. There was lit-

tle formality about Wilson's Scouts. The men at our farm were
part of a regiment, but more than that they were a brother-
hood. They called their captain "Captain Dennis" or just Dennis. Wilson himself, the settler of Machakos who had first
brought them together was simply "F.O.B." because those were
his initials.

Captain Dennis took the Baron out of his stable one morning, and two of the other men got their horses, and when they
were all saddled and bridled—while I leaned against the stable door watching the Baron with what must have been wistful
eyes—Captain Dennis led the big gelding over to me and
handed me the reins. The captain was a lanky man with fierce
grey eyes and a warm smile that laughed at their fierceness—
and I think at me as well.

He said, "You've been watching the Baron like that for
weeks and I can't stand it. We're going to shoot kongonis with
revolvers from horseback, and you're coming along."

I had a currycomb in my hand and I turned without saying
anything and hung the comb on its peg in the stable. When I
came out again my father was standing next to the captain
with a revolver in his hand. It was a big revolver, and when my
father gave it to me he said:

"It's a little heavy, Beryl, but then you never had much fun
with toys. What the captain can't teach you, the Baron will. It
doesn't matter if you don't hit a kongoni, but don't come back
without having learned something—even if it's the knowledge that you can't shoot from horseback."

The captain smiled, and so did my father. Then he kissed
me and I mounted the Baron and we rode away from the
farm—the captain, two cavalry men, and myself—through
some low hills and down into the Rongai Valley, where the
kongonis were.

To say that it was a clear day is to say almost nothing of that country. Most of its days were clear as the voices of the birds that unfailingly coaxed each dawn away from the night. The days were clear and many-colored. You could sit in your saddle and look at the huge mountains and at the river valleys, green, and aimless as fallen threads on a counterpane—and you could not count the colors or know them, because some were nameless. Some colors you never saw again, because each day the light was different, and often the colors you saw yesterday never came back.

But none of this meant much to me that morning. The revolver slung at my waist in a rawhide holster, the broad, straight backs of the cavalrymen riding ahead, the confident pace of the Baron—all these made me feel very proud, but conscious of my youth, smaller, even, than I was.

We hit the bowl of the valley, and in a little while the captain raised his hand, and we looked east into the sun and saw a herd of game about a mile away, feeding in the yellow grass. I had hunted enough on foot to know the tricks: move upwind toward your quarry; keep the light behind you if you can; fan out; be quiet; if there is cover, use it. The captain nodded to me and I waved a hand to show that I would be all right by myself, and then we began to circle, each drifting away from the others, but still joined in the flanking maneuver.

The grass in the Rongai Valley is waist-high and it does not take much of a rise in the plain to hide a man and his horse. In a moment the Baron and I were hidden, and so were the men hidden from us, but the herd of game was just there toward the sun, gathered in a broad clearing—perhaps five thousand head of kongonis, zebras, wildebeests, and oryxes grazing together.

I rode loose-reined, giving the brown gelding his head,

watching his small alert ears, his great bowed neck, feeling the strength of his forthright stride—and I felt that he was hunting with me. He moved with stealth, in easy silence, and I dropped my hand to the revolver, self-consciously, and realized that it was really I who was hunting with him.

He was not an excitable horse, yet he seemed to become even more calm as the distance between the game and ourselves narrowed, while I grew more tense. I sat more rigidly upon the back of the Baron than anyone should ever sit upon the back of any horse, but I had the vanity of youth; I was not to be outdone—not even by soldiers.

By the time the identity of the game had become clear— the horns of oryxes reflecting sunlight like drawn rapiers, the ungainly bulk of wildebeests, zebras flaunting their elaborate camouflage, eland and kongonis in the hundreds—by the time the outlines of their bodies had become distinct to my eyes, I was so on fire with anticipation that I had forgotten my companions.

The Baron and I took advantage of what cover there was and crept up on the outer fringe of the herd until we could smell the dust they stirred to motion with their hooves. Then the Baron stopped and I leaned forward in the saddle. I was breathing unevenly, but the Baron scarcely breathed at all.

Not a hundred yards away, a kongoni stood in long grass, half buried in it. The sun was on him, playing over his sleek fawn coat, and he looked like a beast carved from teakwood and polished by age. He was motionless, he was still, he was alert. High in the shoulders, the line that ran sloping to his hips was scarcely curved, and it forewarned us of his strength and his speed.

It didn't occur to me that I might have been wiser in choosing a smaller animal. One half as big would have been faster than most horses, with perhaps more endurance, but this one was a challenge. I could not resist. In a quick instant of apprehension I peered in all directions, but there was no one near. There were only the Baron, the kongoni, and myself, none of us moving, none of us breathing. Not even the grass moved, and if there were birds they were motionless too.

Leaning low over the Baron's crest, I begin to whisper, smothering my excitement in broken phrases. I ease the reins forward, giving him full head, pressing my hands upon his neck, talking to him, telling him things he already knows: "He's big! He's the biggest of all. He's out of the herd; he's alone, he's ours! Careful, careful!"

The Baron is careful. He sees what I see, he knows more than I know. He tilts his ears, his nostrils distend ever so slightly, the muscles of his shoulders tighten under his skin like leather straps. The tension is so great that it communicates itself to the kongoni. His head comes up and he trembles, he smells the air, he is about to plunge.

"Now!"

The word bursts from my lips because I can no longer contain it; it shatters the stillness. Frightened birds dart into the air, the kongoni leaps high and whirls, but we are off—we are onto him, we are in full gallop, and as the tawny rump of our prey fades into the tawny dust that springs from his heels, I am no longer a girl riding a horse; I am part of the dust, part of the wind in my face, part of the roar of the Baron's hooves, part of his courage, and part of the fear in the kongoni's heart. I am part of everything and it seems that nothing in the world can ever change it.

We run, we race. The kongoni streaks for the open plain. Somewhere to the left there is the drumming of a thousand hooves and the voices of men—angry men with a right to be angry. I have committed the unpardonable; I have bolted their game, but I can't help it.

We're on our own now—the Baron and I—and no sense of guilt can stop us.

We gain, we lose, we hold it even. I grope for the revolver at my thigh and pull it from its sheath. I have used one before, but not like this. Always before it has been heavy in my hand, but now it is weightless; now it fits my hand. Now, I think, I cannot miss.

Rocks, anthills, leleshwa bush, thorn trees—all rush past my eyes, but I do not see them; they are swift streaks of color, unreal and evanescent. And time does not move. Time is a marble moment. Only the Baron moves, his long muscles responding to his will, surging in steady, driving rhythm.

Closer, closer. Without guidance the Baron veers to the left, avoiding the dust that envelops the racing kongoni, exposing him to my aim—and I do aim. I raise the gun to shoulder height, my arm sways, I lower it. No. Too far, I can't get a bead. Faster! It's no good just shooting. I've got to hit his heart. Faster! I do not speak the word; I only frame it on my lips, because the Baron knows. His head drops ever so slightly and he stretches his neck a bit more. Faster? There, you have it—this is faster!

And it is. I raise my arm again and fire twice and the kongoni stumbles. I think he stumbles. He seems to sway, but I am not sure. Perhaps it is imagination, perhaps it is hope. At least he swerves. He swerves to the right, but the Baron outgenerals him; the Baron is on his right flank before I can shift my weight in the saddle.

Then something happens. I want to shoot again, but I can't—there's nothing to shoot at. He's gone—our kongoni's gone. He's disappeared as if his particular god had that moment given him wings. The Baron slows, my hand drops to my side and I mumble my frustration, staring ahead.

It's a *donga*, of course—a pit in the plain, deeper than most, crowded with high grass, its sides steep as walls. Our prize has plunged into it, been swallowed in it, and there is nothing to do except to follow.

That's my impulse, but not the Baron's. He looks from side to side, sudden suspicion in his manner, tension in his body. He slows his pace to scarcely more than a canter and will not be urged. At the rim of the *donga* he almost stops. It is steep, but in the high grass that clothes it I can see the wake of the kongoni, and I am impatient.

"There! Get onto him!"

For the first time I slap the Baron with the flat of my hand, coaxing him forward. He hesitates, and there is so little time to waste. Why is he failing me? Why stop now? I am disappointed, angry. I can't return empty-handed. I won't.

"Now then!"

My heels rap sharply against his ribs, my hand is firmer on the reins, my revolver is ready—and the Baron is a soldier. He no longer questions me; surefooted and strong, half walking, half sliding, he plunges over the rim of the *donga* at such an angle that I brace myself in my stirrups and shut my eyes against the plumes of dust we raise. When it is gone, we are on level ground again, deep in grass still studded with morning dew— and the path of the kongoni is clear before us, easy to see, easy to follow.

We have lost time, but this is no place for speed. Our prey is hiding, must be hiding. Now, once more, we stalk; now we hunt. Careful. Quiet. Look sharply, watch every moving thing; gun ready, hands ready.

I'm ready, but not the Baron. His manner has changed. He is not with me. I can feel it. He responds, but he does not anticipate my will. Something concerns him, and I'm getting nervous too—I'm catching it from him. It won't do. It's silly.

I look around. On three sides we are surrounded by steep banks easier to get down than up—and just ahead there's nothing but bush and high grass that you can't see into. Even so there's a way out—straight ahead through the bush. That's where the kongoni went—it's where we'll go.

"Come on!"

I jab the Baron's ribs once more and he takes a step forward—a single step—and freezes. He does not tremble. With his ears and his eyes and by the sheer power of his will, he forces me into silence, into rigidity, into consciousness of danger.

I feel and see it at the same moment. Wreathed in leaves of shining grass, framed in the soft green garland of the foliage, there is an immense black head into which are sunk two slowly burning eyes. Upon the head, extending from it like lances fixed for battle, are the two horns of a buffalo. I am young, but I am still a child of Africa—and I know that these, without any question, are Africa's most dreaded weapon.

Nor is our challenger alone. I see that not one but a dozen buffalo heads are emerging from the bush, across our path like links in an indestructible chain—and behind us the walls of the _donga_ are remote and steep and friendless. Instinctively I raise my revolver, but as I raise it I realize that it won't help. I know that even a rifle wouldn't help. I feel my meagre store of courage dwindle, my youthful bravado becomes a whisper less audible than my pounding heart. I do not move, I cannot. Still grasping the reins, but unaware of them, the fingers of my left hand grope for the Baron's mane and cling there. I do not utter them, but the words are in my heart: I am afraid. I can do nothing. I depend on you!

Now, as I remember that moment and write it down, I am three times older than I was that day in the *donga*, and I can humor my ego, upon occasion, by saying to myself that I am three times wiser. But even then I knew what African buffaloes were. I knew that it was less dangerous to come upon a family of lions in the open plain than to come upon a herd of buffaloes, or to come upon a single buffalo; everyone knew it— everyone except amateur hunters who liked to roll the word "lion" on their lips. Few lions will attack men unless they are goaded into it; most buffaloes will. A lion's charge is swift and often fatal, but if it is not, he bears no grudge. He will not stalk you, but a buffalo will. A buffalo is capable of mean cunning that will match the mean cunning of the men who hunt him, and every time he kills a man he atones for the death at men's hands of many of his species. He will gore you, and when you are down, he will kneel upon you and grind you into the earth.

I remember that as I sat on the Baron's back the things I had heard about buffaloes swept swiftly into my mind. I remember fingering the big revolver, suddenly becoming heavy in my hand, while the buffaloes moved closer in strategic order.

They stood in an almost mathematical semicircle across the only avenue of escape from the *donga*. They did not gather together for the charge, they did not hurry. They did not have to. They saw to it that every loophole was blocked with their horns, and it seemed that even the spaces between their bodies were barred to us by the spears of light that bristled from their bright, black hides. Their eyes were round and small and they burned with a carnelian fire. They moved upon us with slow leisurely steps, and the intensity of their fury was hypnotic. I could not move.

I would not think, because to think was to realize that behind us there was only a wall of earth impossible to climb in time.

As the nearest bull raised his head, preliminary to the final charge, I raised my revolver and with strange detachment, watched my own hand tremble. It wasn't any good. Thinking of my father, fear changed to guilt and then back to fear again, and then to resignation. All right—come on, then. Let's get it over. It's happened to lots of others and now it's going to happen to me. But I had forgotten my companion. All this time the Baron had not moved. Yet neither had he trembled, nor made a sound.

You can find many easy explanations for the things that animals do. You can say that they act out of fear, out of panic, that they cannot think or reason. But I know that this is wrong; I know now that the Baron reasoned, though what he did at the precise instant of our greatest danger seemed born more of terror than of sense.

He whirled, striking a flame of dust from his heels; he reared high into the air until all his weight lay upon his great haunches, until his muscles were tightened like springs. Then he sprang toward the farthest, steepest wall—while behind us came the drumming, swelling thunder of the herd.

For perhaps a hundred yards the *donga* was broad and flat, and then it ended. I remember that the wall of earth loomed so closely in front of my eyes that they were blinded by it. I saw nothing, but just behind us I could hear the low, the almost soothing undertones of destruction. There was a confident, an all-but-casual quality in the sound; not hurried, hardly in crescendo, not even terrifying, just steady—and inescapable.

Another minute, I thought—a whole minute at least. It's a lot of time; it's sixty seconds. You can do a lot of living in sixty seconds.

And then the Baron turned. I do not know how he turned— I do not know how, running at such speed, he could have turned so swiftly and so cleanly—and I do not know how it was that I stayed in the saddle. I do know that when, at a distance of less than a hundred feet, we faced the onrushing buffaloes once more, they had been beaten, outgeneralled, frustrated; they had lost their battle. An instant ago they had presented an impassable barrier, but now their ranks were spread; now their line was staggered and there were spaces between their beautiful, embracing horns that not one but two horses might have galloped through.

The Baron chose the widest breach and sprinted. He moved toward the open end of the *donga* in great exultant leaps, springing like a reedbuck, laughing in his heart. And when the *donga* was far behind us and the sun was hot on our backs and sweat stood on the Baron's flanks, we came slowly up the wagon track that led to the farm.

I remember that my father and Captain Dennis were talking near the doorway of our house when I rode by, and it may have been that they were smiling; I am not sure. But at least I said nothing and they said nothing, and in a few days all the soldiers left, and it was not until five years had passed that I heard the Baron's name again.

My father spoke it first. We sat at our table one night, and with us sat the colonel of the East African Mounted Rifles. He was not an imposing man; he was red-faced and he looked a little like the colonels in the cartoons you used to see, though of course he was out of uniform.

The war was over and the men had returned to their farms—or some men had. Only a handful of Wilson's Scouts survived, and the colonel and my father talked about that, and then my father asked about Captain Dennis, and the colonel's face got redder. At least he made a grimace with his lips that could only have meant displeasure.

"Dennis," he said, "ah, yes. We had a lot of confidence in him, but he proved a fool. Went dotty over some horse."

My father and I looked at each other. "The Baron," my father said.

The colonel nodded. "That was it. The Baron—big brute with a head like a cartridge case. I remember him."

"What happened?" said my father.

The colonel coughed. He flipped a large hand over on the table and shrugged. "One of those things. CO sent Dennis through von Lettow's lines one night to pick up a spot of news. It was south of Kilimanjaro. Not nice country, but he got through on that clumsy half-breed of his—or almost got through, that is."

"They got him, did they?" said my father.

"Got him in the face with grenade shrapnel," said the colonel. "Not fatal though. With a little sense he would have made it. He clung to that horse and the horse brought him almost all the way back. Then Dennis went off his chump. Disobeyed orders. Had to be rescued. Blasted fool."

My father nodded but said nothing.

"Blasted fool," repeated the colonel. "He was within a mile of our lines with all the information we wanted—then he quit."

"It seems hard to believe," I said.

"Not at all," said the colonel, looking at me with stern eyes. "It was that horse. The brute suddenly went under. Dennis found he'd been shot in the lung. The Baron went down and Dennis wouldn't leave him—sat there the whole night with his face half shot away, trying first aid, holding the brute's head in his lap." The colonel looked at my father with sudden anger. "He'd disobeyed orders. You see that, don't you?"

My father let a smile, half gay, half sad, twist his lips. "Oh clearly! Orders are orders. No room for sentiment in war. You had Captain Dennis court-martialed, of course?"

A hurricane lamp makes almost no sound, but for a long time after my father's question there was no sound but the sound of our hurricane lamp. It gave a voice to silence—the colonel's silence. He looked at both of us. He looked at the table. Then he stared at the wrinkled palms of his clumsy hands until we thought he would never utter another word, but he did.

He stood up. "It took a little time," he said, "but finally Dennis recovered—the Baron died with his head toward our guns. In the end I had them both decorated for bravery beyond the call of duty—the captain and his horse. You see," the colonel added angrily, "I'm afraid I'm a blasted fool myself."

The Splendid Outcast

"The Splendid Outcast" is a fascinating insight into the world of horse-sales and is based on a real event. The horse whom Beryl calls Rigel in her story (after Rigel Beta Orionis, a star particularly visible in the night skies of Kenya) was actually Messenger Boy.

During 1928, shortly after Beryl married the wealthy young aristocrat Mansfield Markham, the couple were in England on honeymoon. Beryl was already a successful trainer, having the winners of the classic Kenya St. Leger and several feature-races as well as numerous minor winners to her credit. She was anxious to improve the bloodline of the horses in her stable and when Messenger Boy was entered for auction at Newmarket, she went with Mansfield to bid for him.

Messenger Boy's breeding was even more impressive than that of Rigel. His sire was Hurry On, winner of the St. Leger in 1916. Never beaten on the turf, Hurry On sired three Derby winners and his trainer, the great Fred Darling, always regarded him as the best horse he had ever trained. To add to this, Messenger Boy's dam was Fifinella, the last filly to win the English Derby and she also won the Oaks in that same year (1916). It would be difficult to envisage a more perfect pedigree and under normal circumstances a foal from this union should have fetched a huge sum at auction, probably even beyond Mansfield's resources.

[First published in *Saturday Evening Post*, September 1944.]

The chestnut colt foaled in 1924 and though showing great promise was a difficult horse to ride and manage. Vicious and unpredictable, in 1927 he killed his groom and attacked Fred Darling, injuring the latter so badly that he was in hospital for weeks. Darling later said that Messenger Boy was one of the few truly insane horses he ever came across during his career.

Mansfield had severe misgivings but Beryl was delighted when she acquired the horse for the remarkably low price of "several hundred pounds." Mansfield told his nephew, Sir Charles Markham, that within weeks of the horse's arrival in Kenya Beryl was using him as a daily hack. Beryl told her friend Doreen Bathurst Norman that she had "simply turned the horse out into a field for a week or so and then got on and rode it," but later she confessed, "Well, he was a bit of a handful at first."

Messenger Boy went on to become one of the leading sires in Kenya racing.

———————

The stallion was named after a star, and when he fell from his particular heaven, it was easy enough for people to say that he had been named too well. People like to see stars fall, but in the case of Rigel, it was of greater importance to me. To me and to one other—to a little man with shabby cuffs and a wilted cap that rested over eyes made mild by something more than time.

It was at Newmarket, in England, where, since Charles I instituted the first cup race, a kind of court has been held for the royalty of the turf. Men of all classes come to Newmarket for the races and for the December sales. They come from everywhere—some to bet, some to buy or sell, and some merely to offer homage to the resplendent peers of the Stud Book, for the sport of kings may, after all, be the pleasure of every man.

December can be bitterly cold in England, and this December was. There was frozen sleet on buildings and on trees, and I remember that the huge Newmarket track lay on the downs below the village like a noose of diamonds on a tarnished mat. There was a festive spirit everywhere, but it was somehow lost on me. I had come to buy new blood for my stable in Kenya, and since my stable was my living, I came as serious buyers do, with figures in my mind and caution in my heart. Horses are hard to judge at best, and the thought of putting your hoarded pounds behind that judgement makes it harder still.

I sat close on the edge of the auction ring and held my breath from time to time as the bidding soared. I held it because the casual mention of ten thousand guineas in payment for a horse or for anything else seemed to me wildly beyond the realm of probable things. For myself, I had five hundred pounds to spend and, as I waited for Rigel to be shown, I remember that I felt uncommonly maternal about each pound. I waited for Rigel because I had come six thousand miles to buy him, nor was I apprehensive lest anyone should take him from me; he was an outcast.

Rigel had a pedigree that looked backward and beyond the pedigrees of many Englishmen—and Rigel had a brilliant record. By all odds, he should have brought ten thousand guineas at the sale, but I knew he wouldn't, for he had killed a man.

He had killed a man—not fallen upon him, nor thrown him in a playful moment from the saddle, but killed him dead with his hooves and with his teeth in a stable. And that was not all, though it was the greatest thing. Rigel had crippled other men and, so the story went, would cripple or kill still more, so long as he lived. He was savage, people said, and while he could not be hanged for his crimes, like a man, he could be shunned as criminals are. He could be offered for sale. And yet, under the implacable rules of racing, he had been warned off the turf for life—so who would buy?

Well, I for one—and I had supposed there would not be

two. I would buy if the price were low enough, because I had youth then, and a corresponding contempt for failure. It seemed probable that in time and with luck and with skill, the stallion might be made manageable again, if only for breeding—especially for breeding. He could be gentled, I thought. But I found it hard to believe what I saw that day. I had not known that the mere touch of a hand, could in an instant, extinguish the long-burning anger of an angry heart.

I first noticed the little man when the sale was already well on its way, and he caught my attention at once, because he was incongruous there. He sat a few benches from me and held his lean, interwoven fingers upon his knees. He stared down upon the arena as each horse was led into it, and he listened to the dignified encomiums of the auctioneer with the humble attention of a parishioner at mass. He never moved. He was surrounded by men and women who, by their impeccable clothes and by their somewhat bored familiarity with pounds and guineas, made him conspicuous. He was like a stone of granite in a jeweler's window, motionless and grey against the glitter.

You could see in his face that he loved horses—just as you could see, in some of the faces of those around him, that they loved the idea of horses. They were the cultists, he the votary, and there were, in fact, about his grey eyes and his slender lips, the deep, tense lines so often etched in the faces of zealots and of lonely men. It was the cast of his shoulders, I think, the devotion of his manner that told me he had once been a jockey.

A yearling came into the ring and was bought, and then another, while the pages of catalogues were quietly turned. The auctioneer's voice, clear but scarcely lifted, intoned the virtues of his magnificent merchandise as other voices, responding to

this magic, spoke reservedly of figures: "A thousand guineas
. . . two thousand . . . three . . . four! . . ."

The scene at the auction comes to me clearly now, as if once
again it were happening before my eyes.

"Five, perhaps?" The auctioneer scans the audience expec-
tantly as a groom parades a dancing colt around the arena.
There is a moment of near silence, a burly voice calls, "Five!"
and the colt is sold while a murmur of polite approval swells
and dies.

And so they go, one after another, until the list is small; the
audience thins and my finger traces the name, Rigel, on the
last page of the catalogue. I straighten on my bench and hold
my breath a little, forgetting the crowd, the little man, and a
part of myself. I know this horse. I know he is by Hurry On
out of Bounty—the sire unbeaten, the dam a great steeple-
chaser—and there is no better blood than that. Killer or not,
Rigel has won races, and won them clean. If God and Barclays
Bank stay with me, he will return to Africa when I do.

And there, at last, he stands. In the broad entrance to the
ring, two powerful men appear with the stallion between
them. The men are not grooms of ordinary size; they have
been picked for strength, and in the clenched fist of each is the
end of a chain. Between the chain and the bit there is on the
near side a short rod of steel, close to the stallion's mouth—a
rod of steel, easy to grasp, easy to use. Clenched around the
great girth of the horse, and fitted with metal rings, there is a
strap of thick leather that brings to mind the restraining harness of a madman.

Together, the two men edge the stallion forward. Tall as
they are, they move like midgets beside his massive shoulders.
He is the biggest thoroughbred I have ever seen. He is the

most beautiful. His coat is chestnut, flecked with white, and his mane and tail are close to gold. There is a blaze on his face—wide and straight and forthright, as if by this marking he proclaims that he is none other than Rigel, for all his sins, for all the hush that falls over the crowd.

He is Rigel and he looks upon the men who hold his chains as a captured king may look upon his captors. He is not tamed. Nothing about him promises that he will be tamed. Stiffly, on reluctant hooves, he enters the ring and flares his crimson nostrils at the crowd, and the crowd is still. The crowd whose pleasure is the docile beast of pretty paddocks, the gainly horse of cherished prints that hang upon the finest walls, the willing winner of the race—upon the rebel this crowd stares, and the rebel stares back.

His eyes are lit with anger or with hate. His head is held disdainfully and high, his neck an arc of arrogance. He prances now—impatience in the thudding of his hooves upon the tanbark, defiance in his manner—and the chains jerk tight. The long stallion reins are tightly held—apprehensively held—and the men who hold them glance at the auctioneer, an urgent question in their eyes.

The auctioneer raises his arm for silence, but there is silence. No one speaks. The story of Rigel is known—his breeding, his brilliant victories, and finally his insurgence and his crimes. Who will buy the outcast? The auctioneer shakes his head as if to say that this is a trick beyond his magic. But he will try. He is an imposing man, an experienced man, and now he clears his throat and confronts the crowd, a kind of pleading in his face.

"This splendid animal—" he begins—and does not finish. He cannot finish.

Rigel has scanned the silent audience and smelled the unmoving air, and he—a creature of the wind—knows the indignity of this skyless temple. He seems aware at last of the chains that hold him, of the men who cling forlornly to the heavy reins. He rears from the tanbark, higher and higher still, until his golden mane is lifted like a flag unfurled and defiant. He beats the air. He trembles in his rising anger, and the crowd leans forward.

A groom clings like a monkey to the tightened chain. He is swept from his feet while his partner, a less tenacious man, sprawls ignobly below, and men—a dozen men—rush to the ring, some shouting, some waving their arms. They run and swear in lowered voices; they grasp reins, chains, rings, and swarm upon their towering Gulliver. And he subsides.

With something like contempt for this hysteria, Rigel touches his forehooves to the tanbark once more. He has killed no one, hurt no one, but they are jabbing at his mouth now, they are surrounding him, adding fuel to his fiery reputation, and the auctioneer is a wilted man.

He sighs, and you can almost hear it. He raises both arms and forgoes his speech. "What," he asks with weariness, "am I offered?" And there is a ripple of laughter from the crowd. Smug in its wisdom, it offers nothing.

But I do, and my voice is like an echo in a cave. Still there is triumph in it. I will have what I have come so far to get—I will have Rigel.

"A hundred guineas!" I stand as I call my price, and the auctioneer is plainly shocked—not by the meagerness of the offer, but by the offer itself. He stares upward from the ring, incredulity in his eyes.

He lifts a hand and slowly repeats the price. "I am offered," he says, "one hundred guineas."

There is a hush, and I feel the eyes of the crowd and watch

the hand of the auctioneer. When it goes down, the stallion will be mine.

But it does not go down. It is still poised in midair, white, expectant, compelling, when the soft voice, the gently challenging voice is lifted. "Two hundred!" the voice says, and I do not have to turn to know that the little jockey has bid against me. But I do turn.

He has not risen from the bench, and he does not look at me. In his hand he holds a sheaf of bank notes. I can tell by their color that they are of small denomination, by their rumpled condition that they have been hoarded long. People near him are staring—horrified, I think—at the vulgar spectacle of cash at a Newmarket auction.

I am not horrified, nor sympathetic. Suddenly I am aware that I have a competitor, and I am cautious. I am here for a purpose that has little to do with sentiment, and I will not be beaten. I think of my stable in Kenya, of the feed bills to come, of the syces to be paid, of the races that are yet to be won if I am to survive in this unpredictable business. No, I cannot now yield an inch. I have little money, but so has he. No more, I think, but perhaps as much.

I hesitate a moment and glance at the little man, and he returns my glance. We are like two gamblers bidding each against the other's unseen cards. Our eyes meet for a sharp instant—a cold instant.

I straighten and my catalogue is crumpled in my hand. I moisten my lips and call, "Three hundred!" I call it firmly, steadily, hoping to undo my opponent at a stroke. It is a wishful thought.

He looks directly at me now, but does not smile. He looks at me as a man might look at one who bears false witness against him, then soundlessly he counts his money and bids again, "Three fifty!"

The interest of the crowd is suddenly aroused. All these people are at once conscious of being witnesses, not only before an auction, but before a contest, a rivalry of wills. They shift in their seats and stare as they might stare at a pair of duelists, rapiers in hand.

But money is the weapon, Rigel the prize. And prize enough, I think, as does my adversary.

I ponder and think hard, then decide to bid a hundred more. Not twenty, not fifty, but a hundred. Perhaps by that I can take him in my stride. He need not know there is little more to follow. He may assume that I am one of the casual ones, impatient of small figures. He may hesitate, he may withdraw. He may be cowed.

Still standing, I utter, as indifferently as I can, the words, "Four fifty!" and the auctioneer, at ease in his element of contention, brightens visibly.

I am aware that the gathered people are now fascinated by this battle of pounds and shillings over a stallion that not one of them would care to own. I only hope that in the heat of it some third person does not begin to bid. But I need not worry; Rigel takes care of that.

The little jockey has listened to my last offer, and I can see that he is already beaten—or almost, at least. He has counted his money a dozen times, but now he counts it again, swiftly, with agile fingers, as if hoping his previous counts had been wrong.

I feel a momentary surge of sympathy, then smother it. Horse training is not my hobby. It is my living. I wait for what I am sure will be his last bid, and it comes. For the first time, he rises from his bench. He is small and alone in spirit, for the glances of the well-dressed people about him lend him nothing. He does not care. His eyes are on the stallion and I can see that there is a kind of passion in them. I have seen that expression before—in the eyes of sailors appraising a comely ship, in the eyes of pilots sweeping the clean, sweet contours of a plane. There is reverence in it, desire—and even hope.

The little man turns slightly to face the expectant auctioneer, then clears his throat and makes his bid. "Four eighty!" he calls, and the slight note of desperation in his voice is unmistakable, but I force myself to ignore it. Now, at last, I tell myself, the prize is mine.

The auctioneer receives the bid and looks at me, as do a hundred people. Some of them, no doubt, think I am quite mad or wholly inexperienced, but they watch while the words "Five hundred" form upon my lips. They are never uttered.

Throughout the bidding for Rigel, Rigel has been ignored. He has stood quietly enough after his first brief effort at freedom; he has scarcely moved. But now, at the climax of the sale, his impatience overflows, his spirit flares like fire, his anger bursts through the circle of men who guard him. Suddenly, there are cries, shouts of warning, the ringing of chains and the cracking of leather, and the crowd leaps to its feet. Rigel is loose. Rigel has hurled his captors from him and he stands alone.

It is a beautiful thing to see, but there is terror in it. A thoroughbred stallion with anger in his eye is not a sight to entrance anyone but a novice. If you are aware of the power and the speed and the intelligence in that towering symmetrical body, you will hold your breath as you watch it. You will know that the teeth of a horse can crush a bone, that hooves can crush a man. And Rigel's hooves have crushed a man.

He stands alone, his neck curved, his golden tail a battle plume, and he turns, slowly, deliberately, and faces the men he has flung away. They are not without courage, but they are without resource. Horses are not tamed by whips or by blows.

The strength of ten men is not so strong as a single stroke of a hoof; the experience of ten men is not enough, for this is the unexpected, the unpredictable. No one is prepared No one is ready.

The words "Five hundred" die upon my lips as I watch, as I listen. For the stallion is not voiceless now. His challenging scream is shrill as the cry of winter wind. It is bleak and heartless. His forehooves stir the tanbark. The auction is forgotten.

A man stands before him—a man braver than most. He holds nothing in his hands save an exercise bat; it looks a feeble thing, and is. It is a thin stick bound with leather—enough only to enrage Rigel, for he has seen such things in men's hands before. He knows their meaning. Such a thing as this bat, slight as it is, enrages him because it is a symbol that stands for other things. It stands, perhaps, for the confining walls of a darkened stable, for the bit of steel, foreign, but almost everpresent in his mouth, for the tightened girth, the command to gallop, to walk, to stop, to parade before the swelling crowd of gathered people, to accept the measured food gleaned from forbidden fields. It stands for life no closer to the earth than the sterile smell of satin on a jockey's back or the dead wreath hung upon a winner. It stands for servitude. And Rigel has broken with his overlords.

He lunges quickly, and the man with a bat is not so quick. He lifts the pathetic stick and waves it in desperation. He cries out, and the voice of the crowd drowns his cry. Rigel's neck is outstretched and straight as a sabre. There is dust and the shouting of men and the screaming of women, for the stallion's teeth have closed on the shoulder of his forlorn enemy.

The man struggles and drops his bat, and his eyes are sharp with terror, perhaps with pain. Blood leaves the flesh of his face, and it is a face grey and pleading, as must be the faces of those to whom retribution is unexpected and swift. He beats against the golden head while the excitement of the crowd mounts against the fury of Rigel. Then reason vanishes. Clubs, whips, and chains appear like magic in the ring, and a regiment of men advance upon the stallion. They are angry men, brave in their anger, righteous and justified in it. They advance, and the stallion drops the man he has attacked, and the man runs for cover, clutching his shoulder.

I am standing, as is everyone. It is a strange and unreal thing to see this trapped and frustrated creature, magnificent and alone, away from his kind, remote from the things he understands, face the punishment of his minuscule masters. He is, of course, terrified, and the terror is a mounting madness. If he could run, he would leave this place, abandoning his fear and his hatred to do it. But he cannot run. The walls of the arena are high. The doors are shut, and the trap makes him blind with anger. He will fight, and the blows will fall with heaviness upon his spirit, for his body is a rock before these petty weapons.

The men edge closer, ropes and chains and whips in determined hands. The whips are lifted, the chains are ready; the battle line is formed, and Rigel does not retreat. He comes forward, the whites of his eyes exposed and rimmed with carnelian fire, his nostrils crimson.

There is a breathless silence, and the little jockey slips like a ghost into the ring. His eyes are fixed on the embattled stallion. He begins to run across the tanbark and breaks through the circle of advancing men and does not stop. Someone clutches at his coat, but he breaks loose without turning, then slows to an almost casual walk and approaches Rigel alone. The men do not follow him. He waves them back. He goes forward, steadily, easily and happily, without caution, without fear, and Rigel whirls angrily to face him.

Rigel stands close to the wall of the arena. He cannot retreat. He does not propose to. Now he can focus his fury on this insignificant David who has come to meet him, and he does. He lunges at once as only a stallion can—swiftly, invincibly, as if escape and freedom can be found only in the destruction of all that is human, all that smells human, and all that humans have made.

He lunges and the jockey stops. He does not turn or lift a hand or otherwise move. He stops, he stands, and there is silence everywhere. No one speaks; no one seems to breathe. Only Rigel is motion. No special hypnotic power emanates from the jockey's eyes; he has no magic. The stallion's teeth are bared and close, his hooves are a swelling sound when the jockey turns. Like a matador of nerveless skill and studied insolence, the jockey turns his back on Rigel and does not walk away, and the stallion pauses.

Rigel rears high at the back of the little man, screaming his defiant scream, but he does not strike. His hooves are close to the jockey's head, but do not touch him. His teeth are sheathed. He hesitates, trembles, roars wind from his massive lungs. He shakes his head, his golden mane, and beats the ground. It is frustration—but of a new kind. It is a thing he does not know—a man who neither cringes in fear nor threatens with whips or chains. It is a thing beyond his memory perhaps—as far beyond it as the understanding of the mare that bore him.

Rigel is suddenly motionless, rigid, suspicious. He waits, and the grey-eyed jockey turns to face him. The little man is calm and smiling. We hear him speak, but cannot understand

his words. They are low and they are lost to us—an incanta-
tion. But the stallion seems to understand at least the spirit if
not the sense of them. He snorts, but does not move. And now
the jockey's hand goes forward to the golden mane—neither
hurriedly nor with hesitance, but unconcernedly, as if it had
rested there a thousand times. And there it stays.

There is a murmur from the crowd, then silence. People
look at one another and stir in their seats—a strange self-
consciousness in their stirring, for people are uneasy before
the proved worth of their inferiors, unbelieving of the virtue
of simplicity. They watch with open mouths as the giant Rigel, the killer Rigel, with no harness save a head collar, follows
his Lilliputian master, his new friend, across the ring.

All has happened in so little time—in moments. The audience begins to stand, to leave. But they pause at the lift of the
auctioneer's hand. He waves it and they pause. It is all very
well, his gestures say, but business is, after all, business, and Rigel has not been sold. He looks up at me, knowing that I have
a bid to make—the last bid. And I look down into the ring at
the stallion I have come so far to buy. His head is low and close
to the shoulder of the man who would take him from me. He
is not prancing now, not moving. For this hour, at least, he is
changed.

I straighten, and then shake my head. I need only say, "Five
hundred," but the words won't come. I can't get them out. I
am angry with myself—a sentimental fool—and I am disappointed. But I cannot bid. It is too easy—twenty pounds too
little, and yet too great an advantage.

No. I shake my head again, the auctioneer shrugs and turns
to seal his bargain with the jockey.

On the way out, an old friend jostles me. "You didn't really
want him then," he says.

"Want him? No. No, I didn't really want him."

"It was wise," he says. "What good is a horse that's warned off every course in the Empire? You wouldn't want a horse like that."

"That's right. I wouldn't want a horse like that."

We move to the exit, and when we are out in the bright cold air of Newmarket, I turn to my friend and mention the little jockey. "But he wanted Rigel," I say.

And my old friend laughs. "He would," he says. "That man has himself been barred from racing for fifteen years. Why, I can't remember. But it's two of a kind, you see—Rigel and Sparrow. Outlaws, both. He loves and knows horses as no man does, but that's what we call him around the tracks—the Fallen Sparrow."

PART TWO

Brothers Are the Same

This story was written during the final months of World War II. Beryl had moved from New Mexico and was living on a ranch in Elsinore in Southern California. Raoul had just been released from active service and placed on general reserve; it was a period of great personal happiness. This is the first of Beryl's stories that was not written in the first person and the style of writing shows some departures from her earlier work. One can only conjecture how much of it is total fiction and how much based upon a child-hood experience. Perhaps it was based upon some gossip Beryl had heard whispered around the firesides of her African friends.

Although the story "Brothers Are the Same" seems on first consideration to have been written out of her deep knowledge of African culture, Raoul told his friend, John Potter, that he had been obliged to comb a reference library for information on Masai tribal customs which Beryl was not able to provide. It appears the story's plot may have been his, while Beryl pro-vided the background that Raoul wove into the story. This was the first story published under her name for which Beryl was not solely responsible, and it appears to have been very much a joint effort.

Although this story may have been a product of Raoul's fertile imagi-nation it is a compelling character study and there is enough of Beryl's writing style in it to convince me that it was not merely ghostwritten.

And the reader can be sure that Beryl knew firsthand the horror of a

[First published in Collier's, The Weekly Magazine, February 1945.]

lion's attack, the brute strength, the overwhelming sounds and smell, for as a small child she was attacked by the supposedly tame lion belonging to a friend: "What I remember most clearly of the moment that followed," she wrote, "are three things—a scream that was barely a whisper, a blow that struck me to the ground, and, as I buried my face in my arms [I] felt Paddy's teeth close on the flesh of my leg. I remained conscious, but I closed my eyes and tried not to be. It was not so much the pain as it was the sound. The sound of Paddy's roar in my ears will only be duplicated, I think, when the doors of hell slip their wobbly hinges, one day, and give voice and authenticity to the whole panorama of Dante's poetic nightmare" [reprinted by kind permission of the Beryl Markham Estate, from West with the Night *by Beryl Markham].*

They are tall men, cleanly built and straight as the shafts of the spears they carry, and no one knows their tribal history, but there is some of Egypt in their eyes and the look of ancient Greece about their bodies. They are the Masai.

They are the color of worn copper and, with their graceful women, they live on the Serengeti Plain, which makes a carpet at the feet of high Kilimanjaro. In all of Africa there are today no better husbandmen of cattle.

But once they were warriors and they have not forgotten that, nor have they let tradition die. They go armed, and to keep well-tempered the mettle of their men, each youth among them must, when his hour comes, prove his right to manhood. He must meet in combat the only worthy enemy his people recognize—the destroyer of their cattle, the marauding master of the plains—the lion.

Thus, just before the dawning of a day in what these Masai call the Month of the Little Rains, such a youth with such a test before him lay in a cleft of rock and watched the shadowed outlines of a deep ravine. For at least eight of his sixteen years, this youth, this young Temas, had waited for his moment. He had dreamed of it and lived it in a dozen ways—all of them glorious.

In all of the dreams he had confronted the lion with casual courage, he had presented his spear on the charging enemy with steadiness born of brave contempt—and always he had won the swift duel with half a smile on his lips. Always—in the dreams.

Now it was different. Now as he watched the place where the real lion lay, he had no smile.

He did not fear the beast. He was sure that in his bones and in his blood and in his heart he was not afraid. He was Masai, and legend said that no Masai had ever feared.

Yet in his mind Temas now trembled. Fear of battle was a nonexistent thing—but fear of failure could be real, and was. It was real and living—and kept alive by the nearness of an enemy more formidable than any lion—an enemy with the hated name Medoto.

He thought of Medoto—of that Medoto who lay not far away in the deep grass watching the same ravine. Of that Medoto who, out of hate and jealousy over a mere girl, now hoped in his heart that Temas would flinch at the moment of his trial. That was it. That was the thing that kept the spectre of failure dancing in his mind, until already it looked like truth.

There were ten youths hidden about the ravine, and they would stage and witness the coming fight. They had tracked the lion to this, his lair, and when the moment came, they would drive him, angered, upon Temas and then would judge his courage and his skill. Good or bad, that judgement would, like a brand mark, cling to him all his life.

But it was Medoto who would watch the closest for a sign,

a gesture, a breath of fear in Temas. It was Medoto who would spread the word—Medoto who surely would cry "Coward!" if he could.

Temas squirmed under the heavy, unwholesome thought, then lifted his head and pierced the dim light with his eyes. To the east, the escarpment stood like a wall against the rising sun. But to the north and to the west and to the south there were no horizons; the grey sky and the grey plain were part and counterpart, and he was himself a shadow in his cleft of rock.

He was a long shadow, a lean shadow. The *shuka* that he wore was now bound about his waist, giving freedom to his legs and arms. His necklace and bracelets were of shining copper, drawn fine and finely spiraled, and around each of his slender ankles there was a copper chain.

His long hair, bound by beaded threads, was a chaste black column that lay between his shoulders, and his ears were pierced and hung with gleaming pendants. His nose was straight, with nostrils delicately flanged. The bones of his cheeks were high, the ridges of his jaw were hard, and his eyes were long and dark and a little brooding. He used them now to glance at his weapons, which lay beside him—a spear, a rawhide shield. These, and a short sword at his belt, were his armament.

He lowered his glance to the place he watched. The ravine was overgrown with a thicket of thorns and the light had not burst through it yet. When it did the lion within it would wake, and the moment would come.

A feeling almost of hopelessness surged through him. It did not seem that he, Temas, could in this great test prove equal to his comrades. All had passed it; all had earned the warrior's title—and none had faltered. Even Medoto—especially Medoto—had proven brave and more than ready for his cloak of manhood. Songs were sung about Medoto. In the evenings in the *manyatta* when the cattle drowsed and the old men drank their honey wine, the girls would gather, and the young men, too, and they would chant to the heroes of their hearts.

But none chanted to Temas. Not yet. Perhaps they never would—not one of them. Not even . . .

He shook his head in anger. He had not meant to think of her—of Kileghen of the soft, deep-smiling eyes and the reed-buck's grace. Even she, so rightly named after the star Venus, had only last night sung to Medoto, and he to her, laughing the while, as Temas, the yet unproven, had clung to the saving shadows, letting his fury burn. Could she not make up her mind between them? Must it always be first one and then the other?

He saw it all with the eye of his memory—all too clearly. He saw even the sneer of Medoto on the day the elder warrior, the chief of them all, had tendered Temas his spear with the wise words: "Now at last this weapon is your own, but it is only wood and steel and means nothing until it changes to honor, or to shame, within your grasp. Soon we shall know!"

And soon they should! But Medoto had laughed then. Medoto had said, "It seems a heavy spear, my comrade, for one so slight—a big weight for any but a man!" And Temas had made no answer. How could he with Kileghen leaning there against the *boma* as though she heard nothing, yet denying her innocence with that quiet, ever-questing smile? At whom had she smiled? At Medoto for his needless malice—or at Temas for his acceptance of it?

He did not know. He knew only that he had walked away carrying the unstained spear a little awkwardly. And that the joy of having it was quickly dead.

Now he spat on the earth where he rested. He raised a curse against Medoto—a harsh, a bitter curse. But in the midst of it he stiffened and grew tense. Suddenly he lay as still as sleep and watched only the ravine and listened, as to the tone of some familiar silence.

It was the silence of a waking lion, for morning light had breached the thicket, and within his lair the lion was roused.

Within his lair the lion sought wakefulness as suspicion came to him on the cool, unmoving air. Under the bars of sunlight that latticed his flanks and belly, his coat was short and shining. His mane was black and evenly grown. The muscles of his forelegs were not corded, but flat, and the muscles of his shoulders were laminated like sheaths of metal.

Now he smelled men. Now as the sunlight fell in streams upon his sorrel coat and warmed his flanks, his suspicion and then his anger came alive. He had no fear. Whatever lived he judged by strength—or lack of it—and men were puny. And yet the scent of them kindled fire in his brooding eyes and made him contemplate his massive paws.

He arose slowly, without sound—almost without motion—and peered outward through the wall of thorns. The earth was mute, expectant, and he did not break the spell. He only breathed.

The lion breathed and swung his tail in easy, rhythmic arcs and watched the slender figure of a human near him in a cleft of rock.

Temas had risen, too. On one knee now, he waited for the signal of the lifted spears.

Of his ten comrades he could see but two or three—a tuft of warrior's feathers, here and there a gleaming arm. Presently all would leap from the places where they hid, and the Masai battle cry would slash through the silence. And then the lion would act.

But the silence held. The interminable instant hung like a drop that would not fall, and Temas remembered many of the rules, the laws that governed combat with a lion—but not enough, for stubbornly, wastefully, foolishly, his mind nagged at fear of disgrace—fear of failure. Fear of Medoto's ringing laughter in the *manyatta*—of Kileghen's ever-questing smile.

"I shall fail," he thought. "I shall fail before Medoto and, through his eyes, she will see my failure. I must fail," he said, "because now I see that I am trembling."

And he was. His hand was loose upon the long steel spear—too loose, the arm that held the rawhide shield was hot and too unsteady. If he had ever learned to weep he would have wept—had there been time.

But the instant vanished—and with it, silence. From the deep grass, from the shade of anthills, from clustered rocks, warriors sprang like flames, and as they sprang they hurled upon the waiting lion their shrill arrogant challenge, their scream of battle.

Suddenly the world was small and inescapable. It was an arena whose walls were tall young men that shone like worn gold in the sun, and in this shrunken world there were Temas and the lion.

He did not know when or how he had left the rock. It was as if the battle cry had lifted him from it and placed him where he stood—a dozen paces from the thicket. He did not know when the lion had come forward to the challenge, but the lion was there.

The lion waited. The ring of warriors waited. Temas did not move.

His long Egyptian eyes swept around the circle. All was perfect—too perfect. At every point a warrior stood blocking the lion from improbable retreat—and of these Medoto was one. Medoto stood near—a little behind Temas and to the right. His shield bore proud colors of the proven warrior. He was lean and proud, and upon his level stare he weighed each movement Temas made, though these were hesitant and few.

For the lion did not seek escape, nor want it. His shifting yellow eyes burned with even fire. They held neither fear nor fury—only the hard and regal wrath of the challenged tyrant. The strength of either of his forearms was alone greater than the entire strength of any of these men; his speed in the attack was blinding speed, shattering speed. And with such knowledge, with such sureness of himself, the lion stood in the tawny grass, and stared his scorn while the sun rose higher and warmed the scarcely breathing men.

The lion would charge. He would choose one of the many and charge that one. Yet the choice must not be his to make, for through the generations—centuries, perhaps—the code of the Masai decreed that the challenger must draw the lion upon him. By gesture and by voice it can be done. By movement, by courage.

Temas knew the time for this had come. He straightened where he stood and gripped his heavy spear. He held his shield before him, tight on his arm, and he advanced, step by slow step.

The gaze of the lion did not at once swing to him. But every eye was on him, and the strength of one pair—Medoto's—burned in his back like an unhealed scar.

A kind of anger began to run in Temas's blood. It seemed unjust to him that in this crucial moment, at this first great trial of his courage, his enemy and harshest judge must be a witness. Surely Medoto could see the points of sweat that now rose on his forehead and about his lips as he moved upon the embattled lion. Surely Medoto could see—or sense—the hesitance of his advance—almost hear, perhaps, the pounding of his heart!

He gripped the shaft of his spear until pain stung the muscles of his hand. The lion had crouched and Temas stood suddenly within the radius of his leap. The circle of warriors had drawn closer, tighter, and there was no sound save the sound of their uneven breathing.

The lion crouched against the reddish earth, head forward. The muscles of his massive quarters were taut, his body was a drawn bow. And, as a swordsman unsheaths his blade, so he unsheathed his fangs and chose his man.

It was not Temas.

As if in contempt for this confused and untried youth who paused within his reach, the lion's eyes passed him by and fastened hard upon the stronger figure of another, upon the figure of Casaro, a warrior of many combats and countless victories.

All saw it. Temas saw it, and for an instant—for a shameless breath of time—he felt an overwhelming ease of heart, relief, deliverance, not from danger, but from trial. He swept his glance around the ring. None watched him now. All action, all thought was frozen by the duel of wills between Casaro and the beast.

Slowly the veteran Casaro sank upon one knee and raised his shield. Slowly the lion gathered the power of his body for the leap. And then it happened.

From behind Temas, flung by Medoto's hand, a stone no larger than a grain of maize shot through the air and struck the lion.

No more was needed. The bolt was loosed.

But not upon Casaro, for if from choice, the regal prowler of the wilderness had first preferred an opponent worthy of *his* worth, he now, under the sting of a hurled pebble, preferred to kill that human whose hand was guilty.

He charged at once, and as he charged, the young Temas was, in a breath, transformed from doubting boy to man. All fear was gone—all fear of fear—and as he took the charge, a light almost of ecstasy burned in his eyes, and the spirit of his people came to him.

Over the rim of his shield he saw fury take form. Light was blotted from his eyes as the dark shape descended upon him—for the lion's last leap carried him above the shield, the spear, the youth, so that, looking upward from his crouch, Temas, for a sliver of time, was intimate with death.

He did not yield. He did not think or feel or consciously react. All was simple. All now happened as in the dreams, and his mind was an observer of his acts.

He saw his own spear rise in a swift arc, his own shield leap on his bended arm, his own eyes seek the vital spot—and miss it.

But he struck. He struck hard, not wildly or too soon, but exactly at the precise, the ripened moment, and saw his point drive full into the shoulder of the beast. It was not enough. In that moment his spear was torn from his grasp, his shield vanished, claws furrowed the flesh of his chest, ripping deep. The weight and the power of the charge overwhelmed him.

He was down. Dust and blood and grass and the pungent lion smell were mingled, blended, and in his ears an enraged, triumphant roar overlaid the shrill, high human cry of his comrades.

His friends were about to make the kill that must be his. Yet his hands were empty, he was caught, he was being dragged. He had scarcely felt the long crescentic teeth close on his thigh, it had been so swift. Time itself could not have moved so fast.

A lion can drag a fallen man, even a fighting man, into thicket or deep grass with incredible ease and with such speed as to outdistance even a hurled spear. But sometimes this urge to plunder first and destroy later is a saving thing. It saved Temas. That and his Masai sword, which now was suddenly in his hand.

Perhaps pain dulled his reason, but reason is a sluggard ally to any on the edge of death. Temas made a cylinder of his slender body and, holding the sword flat against his leg, he whirled, and whirling, felt the fangs tear loose the flesh of his thigh, freeing it, freeing him. And, as he felt it, he lunged.

It was quick. It was impossible, it was mad, but it was Masai madness, and it was done. Dust clothed the tangled bodies of the lion and the youth so that those who clamored close to strike the saving blows saw nothing but this cloud and could not aim into its formless shape. Nor had they need to. Suddenly, as if _En-Gai_ himself—God and protector of these men of wilderness—had stilled the scene with a lifted hand, all movement stopped, all sound was dead.

The dust was gone like a vanquished shadow, and the great, rust body of the lion lay quiet on the rust-red earth. Over it, upon it, his sword still tight in his hand, the youth lay breathing, bleeding. And, beyond that, he also smiled.

He could smile because the chant of victory burst now like drumbeats from his comrades' throats—the paeans of praise fell on him where he lay, the sun struck bright through shattered clouds; the dream was true. In a dozen places he was hurt, but these would heal.

And so he smiled. He raised himself and, swaying slightly like any warrior weak in sinew but strong in spirit from his wounds, he stood with pride and took his accolade.

And then his smile left him. It was outdone by the broader, harder smile of another—for Medoto was tall and straight before him, and with his eyes and with his lips Medoto seemed to say: "It is well—this cheering and this honor. But it will pass—and we two have a secret, have we not? We know who threw the stone that brought the lion upon you when you stood hoping in your heart that it would charge another. You stood in fear then, you stood in cowardice. We two know this, and no one else. But there is one who might, if she were told, look not to you but to the earth in shame when you pass by. Is this not so?"

Yes, it was so, and Temas, so lately happy, shrank within himself and swayed again. He saw the young Kileghen's eyes and did not wish to see them. But for Medoto's stone, the spear of Temas would yet be virgin, clean, unproved—a thing of futile vanity.

He straightened. His comrades—the true warriors, of which even now he was not one—had in honor to a fierce and vanquished enemy laid the dead lion on a shield and lifted him. In triumph and with songs of praise (mistaken praise!) for Temas, they were already beginning their march toward the waiting *manyatta.*

Temas turned from his field of momentary triumph, but Medoto lingered at his side.

And now it will come, Temas thought. Now what he has said with his eyes, he will say with his mouth, and I am forced to listen. He looked into Medoto's face—a calm, unmoving face—and thought: It is true that this, my enemy, saw the shame of my first fear. He will tell it to everyone—and to her.

So, since I am lost, it is just as well to strike a blow against him. I am not so hurt that I cannot fight at least once more.

His sword still hung at his side. He grasped it now and said, "We are alone and we are enemies. What you are about to charge me with is true—but, if I was a coward before the lion, I am not a coward before you, and I will not listen to sneering words!"

For a long moment, Medoto's eyes peered into the eyes of Temas. The two youths stood together on the now deserted plain and neither moved. Overhead the sun hung low and red and poured its burning light upon the drying grass, upon the thorn trees that stood in lonely clusters, upon the steepled shrines of drudging ants. There was no sound of birds, no rasping of cicada wings, no whispering of wind.

And into this dearth, into this poverty of sound, Medoto cast his laugh. His lips parted, and the low music of his throat was laughter without mirth; there was sadness in it, a note of incredulity, but not more, not mockery, not challenge.

He stared into the proud unhappy face of Temas. He plunged the shaft of his spear into the earth and slipped the shield from his arm. At last he spoke.

He said, "My comrade, we who are Masai know the saying: 'A man asks not the motives of a friend, but demands reason from his enemy.' It is a just demand. If, until now, I have seemed your enemy, it was because I feared you would be braver than I, for when I fought my lion my knees trembled and my heart was white—until that charge was made. No one knew that, and I am called Medoto, the unflinching, but I flinched. I trembled."

He stepped closer to Temas. He smiled. "It is no good to lie," he said. "I wanted you to fail, but when I saw you hesitate I could not bear it because I remembered my own hour of fear.

It was then I threw the stone—not to shame you, but to save you from shame—for I saw that your fear was not fear of death, but fear of failure—and this I understood. You are a greater warrior than I—than any—for who but the bravest would do what you have done?" Medoto paused and watched a light of wonderment kindle in Temas's eye. The hand of Temas slipped from his sword, his muscles relaxed. Yet, for a moment, he did not speak, and as he looked at Medoto, it was clear to both that the identical thought, the identical vision, had come to each of them. It was the vision that must and always will come to young men everywhere, the vision of a girl.

Now this vision stood between them, and nothing else. But it stood like a barrier, the last barrier.

And Medoto destroyed it. Deliberately, casually, he reached under the folds of his flowing *shuka* and brought from it a slender belt of leather crusted with beads. It was the work and the possession of a girl, and both knew which girl. Kileghen's handiwork was rare enough, but recognized in many places.

"This," said Medoto, "this, I was told to bring, and I was told in these words: 'If in his battle the young Temas proves himself a warrior and a man, make this belt my gift to him so that I may see him wear it when he returns. But if he proves a coward, Medoto, the belt is for you to keep.'"

Medoto looked at the bright gift in his hands. "It is yours, Temas!" He held it out. "I meant to keep it. I planned ways to cheat you of it, but I do not think a man can cheat the truth. I have seen you fight better than I have ever fought, and now this gift belongs to you. It is her wish and between us you are at last her choice." He laid the belt on the palm of Temas's open hand and reached once more for his shield and spear. "We will return now," Medoto said, "for the people are waiting. She is waiting. I will help you walk."

But Temas did not move. Through the sharp sting of his wounds, above his joy in the promise that now lay in his hands, he felt another thing, a curious, swelling pride in this new friendship. He looked into the face of Medoto and smiled, timidly, then broadly. And then he laughed and drew his sword and cut the beaded belt in half.

"No," he said. "If she has chosen, then she must choose again, for we are brothers now and brothers are the same!"

He entwined one half of the severed belt in the arm band of Medoto, and the other half he hung, as plainly, on himself.

"We begin again," he said, "for we are equal to each other, and this is a truth that she must know. She must make her choice on other things but skill in battle, since only men may judge a warrior for his worth!"

It was not far to the *manyatta* and they walked it arm in arm. They were tall together, and strong and young, and somehow full of song. Temas walked brokenly for he was hurt, and yet he sang:

> *Oi-Konyek of the splendid shield*
> *Has heard the lowing of the kine* . . .

And when they entered the gates of the *manyatta*, there were many of every age to welcome Temas, for his lion had been brought and his story told. They cheered and cried his name and led him past the open doors to the peaceful earthen houses to the *singara*, which is the place reserved for warriors.

Medoto did not leave him, nor he Medoto, and it was strange to some to see the enemies transformed and strong in friendship, when yesterday their only bond was hate.

It was strange to one who stood against the *boma* wall, a slender girl of fragile beauty and level, seeking eyes. She was as young as morning, as anticipant. But this anticipation quickly dimmed as she saw the token she had made, one half borne hopefully by Medoto, the other as hopefully carried by Temas!

Both sought her in the gathered crowd, both caught her glance and gave the question with their eyes. Both, in the smug, self-satisfied way of men, swaggered a little.

So the girl paused for an instant and frowned a woman's frown. But then, with musing, lidded eyes, she smiled a woman's smile—and stranger yet, the smile had more of triumph in it, and less of wonder, than it might have had.

PART THREE

The final four stories are based on fictional, mainly romantic, situations of a type in great demand during the war—and immediate postwar—years by a public that dictated a requirement for escapist entertainment. These stories lean heavily on Beryl's African, equine, and aviation background. Though originally published under Beryl's name, the three stories in Part Three were probably ghostwritten by Raoul Schumacher; for the style is clearly identical to that of the handful of short stories published by him. Nevertheless, they will be interesting to admirers of Beryl Markham; her experiences add dimension to the thin plots.

Appointment in Khartoum

The threads of Beryl's own life can be seen in the experiences of the young aviatrix flying what she takes to be a chauvinistic, male passenger across the Sudd. Beryl flew this route many times, and her description of flying through a violent storm and the forced landing may well be grounded in personal experience, for her logbook records such an occurrence during her solo flight to England in 1932.

The heroine of "Appointment in Khartoum" is an American girl, and there is contemporary Allied patriotism as well as romance in the ending of the story, which was written in early 1944 when the war was still at its height. But the slight plot forces one to wonder why Kensing—apparently such a brilliant pilot—could not, himself, have flown to Khartoum.

The *babu* desk clerk was apologetic. He wore a red fez upon his narrow head, and he emphasized his regret by shaking the fez from side to side rhythmically, like a band leaders' baton. No, the plane for Khartoum had not arrived. It would not arrive. The weather was bad. He was immensely, abjectly, miserably sorry, but there was no other available plane in Jerba,

[First published in *Collier's, The National Weekly*, April 1944.]

and would Mr. Kensing be kind enough to sit down and drink some tea?

Mr. Kensing would not. He was tall, and when he leaned over the desk, the *babu* seemed to shrink visibly—fez and all.

"Thank you very much—and blast your tea! I want a plane. I wired for a plane. My business can't wait. Telegraph Nairobi and don't stand there shaking that silly cap!"

The girl in the rawhide chair looked up from her year-old copy of a sports magazine and concluded that the stranger had a foul temper. He was obviously English, plainly in a hurry, and probably connected with the Foreign Office. War had dumped some peculiar people into the heart of Africa— urgent people with a common loathing for delay. They wore their tempers on their sleeves and went around tearing up red tape as if it were confetti.

She looked through the fly-specked window of what was euphemistically, perhaps even sarcastically, called the Hotel Jerba. Had it been called the Jerba Opera House, it would have made as much sense. It was a ten-room corrugated-iron shack with medieval plumbing, and with the Anglo-Egyptian Sudan for a garden. It had an airport with two gently sagging hangars, which now, before the slow stalking wind, were beginning to tremble as if anticipating the impending storm. The plane that had brought the Englishman had gone. No other plane would arrive from Nairobi that day—perhaps not for many days.

She put her magazine aside, wondering somewhat skeptically just how important the young man's business might be. Then she shrugged. It didn't matter.

Or did it? As if she had been made alert by some pinprick of an idea, she sat erect in the chair, then leaned forward, an expression of sudden interest in her face. Perhaps, she thought, just perhaps . . .

She watched the restless stranger pace the floor with enormous strides—enormous, but uneven. His slight limp was apparent enough to her, but he himself ignored it with magnificent disdain. He stared at the little desk clerk who was furiously clicking his telegraph key—and waited.

When the answer came, the *babu* punched it out on a typewriter and handed the sheet to the Englishman, who read it out loud in staccato syllables: ALL PLANES GROUNDED SUGGEST MR. KENSING GET MEREDITH IF POSSIBLE AND AT OWN RISK. SELFRIDGE.

Mr. Kensing crumpled the sheet and swore beautifully, but with British restraint. He lowered his head and crept toward the *babu* as if he were going to pounce. "Meredith, eh? So there is a pilot here! Why the devil didn't you tell me that? Where is this fellow, Meredith? This is wartime. Move!"

The *babu* moved. He moved a little like someone quite lately struck over the head with a sandbag—uncertainly, warily. He came around the desk that was made of crude planking and aimed a brown, unstable finger at the girl in the rawhide chair.

With notable lack of gallantry he said, "That, sir, I am very sorry, please forgive, is this fellow Miss Meredith—a woman, you will observe."

"A woman?" Mr. Kensing uttered the word with plain incredulity, almost with distaste. He took three steps toward Diana Meredith and stared at her, around her, and through her. He wiped his forehead with a very smart blue handkerchief. "I beg your pardon—but are you . . ."

"A woman?" Diana smiled and looked at her trousers. "Don't let the slacks fool you. Skirts would be silly out here."

"I'm sorry. I didn't mean that. I'm looking for a pilot and a plane."

Diana stood up and shook her chestnut hair into place. Her

eyes were about on a level with Grey Kensing's shoulders, and she had to tilt her head upward to speak to him.

"I know," she said. "I couldn't help hearing. I'm a pilot and I have a plane. The war has grounded me, and I've been hoping for a chance." Her voice was confident, but eager. "I thought if I could prove my usefulness . . ." She hesitated, then let the sentence die on her lips.

Grey Kensing was shaking his head a little wearily but with unmistakable firmness. "Terribly sorry, Miss—Meredith is it?—my pilot would have to be a man, of course. Can't trust girls or amateurs, you know, on business matters—war matters. You have the plane. Now if you could suggest some pilot . . . some professional . . ."

Grey Kensing stopped talking abruptly because he had no one to talk to. Diana was halfway to the door before she turned. There was a blaze of anger in her smoke blue eyes, but she kept her voice cool.

"This is Africa," she said. "The facilities are somewhat limited. So is the supply of pilots. I would suggest you cable London—they might send you one."

She didn't slam the door; she closed it quietly and went across the runway, biting her lip and fighting the rising wind.

Professional pilot! For three years, she had flown her one-plane taxi service into almost every corner of central, east, and north Africa under commercial license—until the war had grounded her. Now, thousands of miles from Texas—and home—she was not only useless but had to be reminded of it by an impatient Englishman.

She swung open the door of the small hangar with a good deal more strength than required. Midmorning light poured over the yellow wings and fuselage of her tiny Avian. It was a biplane with an open cockpit, few instruments, and a galaxy of patches that, to Diana, were no indication of weakness, but only so many symbols of character and integrity.

"My dear young lady!"

She swung round with less surprise than annoyance. My dear young lady indeed! She muttered the phrase in her mind. Grey Kensing looked scarcely four years older than she, yet there he stood in the hangar doorway, talking like a character out of a third-rate play—looking like one, too—handsome, and better dressed than made sense in this windy wilderness.

She didn't answer. She waited.

He indicated the Avian with a resigned but disappointed gesture of his hand. "So that's what you call your plane. That's what you expect to get me to Khartoum in—bad weather and all!" He looked angry, even desperate.

Diana nodded. "That," she admitted, "is what I call my plane. I've flown over half of Africa in it and I expect to fly over the other half in the same machine. As for getting to Khartoum in it, I'm sorry I made the suggestion. I could get you there—storm or no storm—but you don't trust women pilots, and that's that. You'll have to excuse me now. I'm closing the hangar." She moved toward the door with quick, determined steps.

Grey Kensing sighed. He moved toward the plane. He said, "Miss Meredith, please don't be coy. I didn't come out here in order to sell whisk brooms. I have a job to do for my government—your government, too, incidentally. It's a small job perhaps, but it's important, and I have got to be in Khartoum by morning. You offered to fly me. I'm accepting the offer. I can't do anything else."

Quite as casually as if he were himself the owner of the Avian—albeit not a proud owner—Grey Kensing tossed a briefcase and a small overnight bag into the locker, then turned again to Diana, whose face bore an expression of mingled bewilderment and fury.

She had concluded that she could either slam the hangar door in his face or swallow her pride for the sake of the chance to get off the ground again. Once she had got him across ths Sudd and safely to Khartoum, he might be generous enough to admit that she could fly. Everything helped. A lot could depend on this one flight. She decided against slamming the hangar door. Instead, she opened it wider, and together, in brittle silence, they pushed the plane out onto the runway.

As she got into her seat behind the instrument board, Diana thought she saw just the glimmer of a smile on Grey Kensing's lips. She wasn't sure, but it seemed to her a challenging smile . . .

If you are a pilot with a morose turn of mind and wish to escape the world, you need only fly north from Jerba. When the great green Sudd begins to crawl under your wings, you have at least escaped the world that men know and walk upon and quarrel over. The Sudd is the dregs of Africa, the backwash of the Nile, a flat never-ending swamp garrisoned by crocodiles. It spreads between Jerba and Malakal. It seems to wait for planes to fall—a vast receptacle, hopeful of misfortune.

To Diana, the Sudd, in any weather, was a nightmare. In a storm it was delirium come true, but any way you looked at it, you were a fool to fly over it if you didn't have to.

She was flying over it and she supposed that she didn't really have to. She sat at the controls of the Avian and told herself that normally, under the promise of such foul weather, she wouldn't have budged from the runway. Still, when you wanted a chance at something, you did strange, even foolhardy things. That was one reason. The other—well, it was hardly clear in her mind, nor was she sure she wanted it to be. She was not going to admit that Grey Kensing's outspoken disbelief of her ability had influenced her for a moment.

She looked to the east and saw the storm clouds rolling toward her like smoke from a burning forest. The familiar stench of the Sudd began to invade the cockpit, and she eased back on the stick and climbed . . .

She was cruising at a hundred miles an hour when the storm hit. At first, there was no rain; it was all wind and darkness. Diana experienced the eerie sensation of seeing the wings of her plane and all else that was visible swallowed in the gloom until she and Grey Kensing seemed borne wholly by magic and the roar of her engine. It was not a new sensation. She and the Avian were intimate with storm, but somehow today it was disquieting.

When the rain came, lightning came with it, ripping the black fabric of the sky, framing the Avian in momentary halos of brilliance and, as abruptly, leaving it to darkness.

Diana was suddenly alone. It was the aloneness of concentration—of swiftly moving hands, of concerned eyes darting from instrument to instrument, of feet, sensitive, steady, alert on the rudder bar—the aloneness of caution, of determination, of competence. She was alone as she had been a thousand times before, and when the bland voice of Grey Kensing came to her through her earphones it was as startling as a hand suddenly placed upon her shoulders.

"How far to Malakal?"

She snorted. Ten minutes of storm and he was already anxious for a runway.

"An hour, I think—maybe more." She had to scream it into the mouthpiece, outshouting both the engine and the thunder, but there was a sharpness in her voice not common to her. She wanted to add, "Maybe two hours—four—six! If you're afraid, we'll turn."

But he wasn't afraid. She knew he wasn't afraid, and even that knowledge vaguely annoyed her; he was simply cold and critical and obsessed with getting to Khartoum.

The storm had risen to its full malevolence, and she felt, as she had often done, the real enmity of the elements—their hatred of men's intrusion into the sky. Wind struck at the little airplane with hammer blows, lightning blinded its eyes, darkness made it blunder on its way. And below it all lay the Sudd.

She worked in silence, neither complaining to herself nor aloud. What disturbed her most was that, after all her countless hours in the air, she was being compelled to prove herself once more—and to a brusque and even arrog nt young man she had never seen before and never wanted to see again.

She put her head out of the cockpit and stared down, but the air was opaque as an angry sea. The guiding ribbon of the Nile had not yet appeared.

A muffled metallic cough—louder to her than thunder had ever been—came to her ears. Of all sounds in the world, this one sound is, to a pilot, the most significant, the most hated, the most feared. Diana couldn't believe it, but there it was. She wouldn't believe it, but it was true. Now at last it had happened. Now, in the full temper of the storm, the Avian was failing her. It was dying on her.

The splutter increased—sharp staccato barkings of the exhaust, the roar of the engine fighting to live, the cough again, the hesitance, the silence amidst sound, the hush of the powerless prop.

She bit her lip, remembering the worn petrolflex that she had not been able to replace. Air in the fuel tube. Airlock. Her fingers closed on the throttle. It was no good. She eased forward on the stick. She had to. They were falling, losing altitude, circling toward the Sudd. She steadied the plane and thrust it into the wind, working for time, but there was no time.

She lifted the speaking tube and said into it, "You had better hang on. We're going down." Her voice was even, but heavy with bitterness—filled with bitterness. There was no fear in it, only admission of defeat and failure.

Under a flash of lightning she saw Grey Kensing leaning forward as if intent upon something in his hands. Then the lightning was gone, and his infuriatingly calm British voice came to her through the earphones: "Swamp underneath, I believe. Bad show, isn't it?"

"Bad show!" Diana blurted it out loud. Did he always respond to everything with moth-eaten English clichés? She thrust her head out of the cockpit as she caught the altimeter reading with the tail of her eye. Two thousand feet and losing altitude fast. She couldn't see anything below. She didn't particularly want to. She knew what was there.

At five hundred feet, she saw what was there—a motionless mat of green scum, steamy with the falling rain, flat as an airport, inviting, beckoning. She circled, keeping the plane aloft almost with the strength of her will, catching the wind, letting it lift her so long as it would.

It was not long. The dead engine was dragging the Avian inexorably earthward, swampward. At a hundred feet, she saw the ridge of shining clay jutting away from the morass and she was suddenly calm. Calm—and angry, and bitter. She had a choice to make; crash on the ridge, or be sucked into the swamp. It didn't matter which, but the first seemed the least ignominious. She said into the speaking tube, "I'm sorry, but this is it!" and began to sideslip. She made a bird of the Avian, spilling air from one wing, then from the other—teetering, sliding on the wind like a falling hawk, dropping.

She had no time to look at Grey Kensing but she was somehow conscious of his poised rigidity as they fell. He was silent, unmoving, vindicated in his distrust of women pilots for whatever satisfaction there was in it. There couldn't be much, she was thinking. And then they struck.

They didn't land, they struck, the little plane hit the clay ridge squarely with both wheels and then skidded, leaped into the air, and struck again. The jolt was more sickening than painful. It hurled Diana forward in her safety belt until she thought the canvas would break. Not once—twice—three times—four. She thought the jolting would never stop, and then, abruptly, it did.

It stopped and, except for the driving rain, there was silence. No other sound. Not even thunder. A terrible silence. A silence of defeat and despair and emptiness.

She looked at Grey Kensing. He didn't turn: he didn't say a word. He wouldn't, she thought. He was unbuckling his safety belt—slowly, methodically, as if they had come down not in the world's most miserable swamp, but on a paved airport lined with lights. He was imperturbable, superior, hateful.

He clambered out of the plane and reached to help Diana, saying nothing.

Manners, she thought, those inbred, meaningless, English manners!

She took his hand and got out and looked at him. His dark hair was ruffled, there was a little trickle of blood on his cheek. Not much, but a little. He pulled a handkerchief out of his pocket and patted the trickle neatly. Then he looked at his watch, at Diana, at the Avian.

"Airlock, I think," he said. "Have you a spanner?" He didn't say, "Are you all right" or "Are you hurt?" Just, "Airlock, I think. Have you a spanner?" It was exactly as if he had said, "Could I bother you for a match?"

Diana opened her mouth, then closed it again. "Spanner?" Well that was English for wrench. He wanted a wrench. This obviously nonmechanical, perfectly groomed young Englishman wanted a wrench.

She wanted to laugh, but before she knew it, she had got the box open and was handing him the wrench.

She wanted to swear, too, but she wasn't very good at it, so she didn't. She walked around the plane peering at every strut and joint and wheel. It was intact. Rugged and tough and ready, the little Avian stood there—one wheel on soft clay, the other on fairly hard ground. Not a scratch on her. There was a devilish, minxlike quality in her tip-tilted attitude. Diana shook her head. Why, of all times, should this have been the time for failure! Why couldn't she have been alone when it happened?

She looked around her. The storm was waning, but the rain had stirred the Sudd until its stench was thick as mist. They were on an island of rain-sleek clay—an island perhaps twelve yards wide and four hundred yards long. Normally the Avian required about six hundred yards for a takeoff—in dry weather. Two hundred yards less meant a lot, especially on a wet surface. Still, there were the doughnut tires. They helped—or were said to, anyway.

She went round to the cowling and saw that it was open and that Grey Kensing's head was under it. He was making a noble effort but probably didn't know a carburetor from a wing flap. Manlike, he thought he had to do something.

She rolled up her sleeves. She had humored his ego long

enough. They were lucky to be alive whether he knew it or not—Khartoum or no Khartoum. If they got out of here, he could spend the rest of his life cursing women pilots and the crates they flew in. It didn't matter anymore. She was dejected and impatient—and worried.

She said, "Better let me handle it. I know the engine."

He said, "Get some tape."

She hesitated, making no effort to stem her annoyance. "Mr. Kensing," she said.

He didn't lift his head, but he lifted his voice. He roared "Tape, dammit!"

A moment later she stood beside him, tight-lipped, furious, groping for effective words and not finding them—but the tape was in her hand. When he said, "Wire," she got it. When he said, "Pliers," she got them. When, finally, after what seemed ages, but was only ten minutes, he turned his grease-stained face toward her and pointed to the cockpit, she got behind the controls without a word. If she had had a word, she couldn't have uttered it. It wouldn't have come.

She had a vision of his explaining his lateness in Khartoum, explaining it in clipped English terms: "Girl pilot—American, I think—best I could do. Put me smack down in the Sudd with a frayed petrolflex—had to fix it myself. Man's job, flying. Shouldn't permit—"

Smothering her resentment, Diana watched him return from his inspection of what had to be the runway. She had looked it over herself, of course, but that had not been enough—not for Grey Kensing. He walked round the cowling and put his hands on the propeller with such confident ease that she did not stop him.

"Contact?" he said.

"Contact!" she snapped.

The engine roared and he got into his seat. He had taken over. He had simply taken over, and there she sat, in her own plane, waiting for a signal to take off.

The astonishing thing was that he confidently expected her to perform the miraculous. He ignored the soft going, the shortness of the run, the direction of the wind. He just lifted his hand, as if flying were child's play, and Diana (like an obedient child) took off.

It was as simple as that; and, as the Avian shook the Sudd from her heels—quite as nonchalantly as Grey Kensing might have done—she told herself that never in her twenty-one years had she disliked anyone so much, unless it was herself at that moment for having left her single chance to prove her mettle behind her on that scum-surrounded ledge.

Malakal for fuel, then Omdurman, and then Khartoum just across the White Nile. No more storm, and the evening sky was blue as heavy glass. The adobe huts of Omdurman stood in the valley like nursery blocks on a green rug. Diana sighed, as she always did when she saw the airport—flat and yellow and capacious as a Texas plain.

She sighed, but with more relief than she had ever done. It was not only the flight that was ended. So too was this enforced companionship with the maddening, arrogant—and yet strangely casual—Grey Kensing.

He had made Khartoum—and with half an hour to spare. Yet, so long as he remembered that flight, he would inevitably recall it as the flight on which a girl pilot—or would-be pilot—had put him down.

When they had landed and he had once more helped her out of the cockpit in that precise and dutiful manner of his, he bowed a little hesitantly, mumbled his thanks, and asked if she needed a lift into town. His hair was tousled, the bruise on his cheek had turned slightly blue, and his shirt had grease on it. Diana decided that, for the first time, he looked eminently human, but she did not dwell upon the discovery.

She shook her head. No. No, thanks. It was nice of him to offer the lift, but she couldn't. Had to get a mechanic on the machine right away. Things to see to . . .

She smiled and he smiled—somewhat painfully it seemed— and then he was gone, walking away from her, tall, erect, overcoming his limp by the sheer pride of his carriage.

Diana watched him for a moment, then leaned against the wing of her plane, pulled off her helmet and let the wind blow idly through her hair. That was that, she thought. Grey Kensing—embodiment of a fine, self-centered man. She wondered why he had bothered to thank her at all. Habit, no doubt. He'd probably thanked bus drivers and doormen in exactly the same way. Mustn't be rude to the working classes, you know!

She thought of the entry she would make in her pilot's logbook: "Jerba to Khartoum—Pilot, Self. Passenger, Grey Kensing." Under "remarks" she would, of course, write: "Forced landing—Sudd," and she would write it with bitterness. Any chance she might have had to fly regularly again, to revive her air service and put it to wartime needs, instead of carrying lion and elephant hunters from place to place, would be gone now.

She sighed and turned to the Avian. She would get a mechanic to repair the petrolflex, and she would return to Jerba in the morning. She was unaccountably depressed, but she couldn't shake it off. She began to check over the plane as was her habit, but she went about it mechanically, almost without interest. When she got to the front cockpit, she glanced at the seat Grey Kensing had occupied, then turned back again.

Something had caught her eye. It was a scrap of white paper, a used envelope crumpled into a ball. It lay on the floor beside the seat.

Diana looked at it, hesitated, then reached into the cockpit. She got the little ball of paper and compressed it in her hand as if to toss it to the ground but she didn't. Something kept her from it. She unfolded the envelope with a childish feeling of guilt and saw there was writing on its back.

It was scrawled, uneven writing, scarcely legible. As she read, she recalled the brief moment when Grey Kensing had sat, head forward, silhouetted by the blazing sky, intent on something in his hands. This then was what it had been.

She made her lips move slowly, though she read in silence, bewildered silence, almost unbelieving silence:

"I wish to make it clear that, should this plane be found wrecked, it will in no way be the fault of the pilot, Miss Meredith. She made the flight altogether at my insistence and has acted with skill and courage. Grey Kensing."

That was all—or Diana thought it was. She stared at the crumpled envelope with blurred eyes. She turned it over and over again in her fingers, but it was not until she had stood there like that for a long time that she noticed the typewritten words on the front of the envelope—the words that had been used by someone to address Grey Kensing—and it was what followed his name that caught her eye. "Grey Kensing," the clean-cut letters spelled, "Grey Kensing, DFC."

Distinguished Flying Cross! She didn't know whether anger, embarrassment, or shame was the uppermost of her emotions. Perhaps it was a combination of the three. Grey Kensing, DFC. A war ace—and she, Diana, had undertaken to show him how to cross the Sudd in a storm! It was worth a laugh, but there was no laughter in her heart. She wanted to crawl into a hotel room and lock the door and just stay there until her Avian was ready to fly back to Jerba once more.

As she stood there, with the gallant and generous note in her hand, a lump came into her throat and would have been followed by tears if she hadn't held them back. It was obvious enough that in the midst of the storm over the Sudd—at the moment when the forced landing had become inevitable—Grey Kensing had thought not so much of his own safety as he had thought of Diana's honor and reputation as a pilot. If, by chance, he had been killed, and she had lived, that little note, scratched out up there in the wild, resentful sky, would have absolved her of his death. All danger over, he had of course thrown the note from the plane but, as nearly always happened, the wind had hurled it back again, back to her.

Grey Kensing, DFC. She repeated the name and, repeating it, found answers to some of the questions in her mind. She knew now that he had been decorated for bravery. She could guess the rest. His limp must be the result of battle injury. He had been retired out of the service and put into civilian work. The gruff manner, the impatience, the seeming rudeness—all these were to cover the disappointment, the bitterness that must come to a fighting man no longer bearing arms, to a pilot no longer able to fly.

She shook herself out of her reverie. An airport attendant had come up, and she went through the routine of presenting her papers and arranging for the care of the plane, then she walked slowly toward one of the shining cars that served the airport as taxis.

She said, "Grand Hotel," to the Egyptian driver—and said it listlessly.

In a few minutes, the driver stopped before a deep veranda

that looked down upon the dreaming Nile, but Diana, who loved the river, did not look at it now. She gave the driver a note and waived the change.

In a few minutes, a Sudanese boy was leading her along the dark, fan-cooled corridor toward her room. She was still in her flying clothes, and a few curious people had stared at her as curious people do, but she was unaware of them.

The Sudanese boy stopped and opened a door, and she was thanking him and fumbling in her pocket for change when another door opened and Grey Kensing stepped into the corridor. He was in fresh clothes and immaculate once more. He came toward her, trying, as always, to hide his modest limp, and Diana thought that his smile had lost its challenge, its gently mocking quality.

He said, "You ought to have come with me. I asked you." Diana nodded and found herself stupidly groping for words. A little impatiently, she handed the waiting boy a few coins, and when he had left and they were alone, she saw that her unsteady fingers had dropped the crumpled envelope that she had found in the plane and that Grey Kensing had stooped to pick it up.

For a moment, she could say nothing. He had recognized it, of course, and was doubtless wondering why she had clung to it all the way from the airport. Nor could she have explained it to him. But she tried. She said, "I—it must have blown back. I'm afraid I read it. It was good of you."

He moved closer to her and looked questioningly into her eyes.

"About the forced landing," she said. "I wanted to make a better showing. I . . ."

His hands were on her shoulders before she could finish— large hands, strong but strangely gentle. He looked down upon her, smiling. The abrupt, cold manner, the icy reserve were suddenly gone, and his eyes were warm. He shook his head.

"No," he said, "I don't see. I didn't write that note out of kindness, but out of simple respect for a fellow flier and a master of the craft. I'd made a mistake in judging you and I had to make it right. That was just the beginning."

He took her arm in his and began to march her solemnly down the corridor and toward the broad veranda busy with white-clad Sudanese boys, tinkling glasses, and uniforms of a dozen nations.

When they were comfortable in the wicker chairs and he had ordered champagne cocktails, he reached across the table and took Diana's hand in his own.

"You see," he explained, "a mistake like mine takes a lot of undoing—weeks, months, years perhaps! It's a big job—even for an Englishman. So big, in fact, I'm going to need an ally."

Diana laughed. "Your traditional ally?" He nodded. "America," he said and lifted his glass to hers.

"Contact?"

"Contact!"

The Nile was silent, and yet as Diana peered through the trees that stood in dutiful attendance upon its banks, the river seemed to glow with a wise and age-old smile—placid, knowing and, beyond all things, content.

_____ Your Heart Will Tell You _____

Juanita, the surprisingly pliant heroine of "Your Heart Will Tell You," flew her airplane into the desert to search for her childhood friend. Beryl could provide the background to this story with complete confidence for she had done the same thing many times in her Avro Avian, searching for fellow aviators whose airplanes had failed to report to their intended destination. However, it is difficult to believe that Beryl would have put herself in the same situation as Juanita, who continued her search even when she knew it meant using up the fuel required to fly to safety.

Perhaps Beryl was repeating the words of her own flying instructor, Tom Campbell Black, in Peter's response to Juanita's suggestion to fly to the rescue, "[It's] a fool's errand so long as there's a rescue party on the way. A good flier never risks the same accident twice. If you want to be good, remember that. You can't fly on your emotions. . . . It's the harebrained pilots that make people mistrust flying, the hero boys full of daredevil nonsense from the last war, all anxious to have their necks broken in another one." It sounds like Tom, careful and precise; but Tom was responsible for many such rescues himself, including that of the famous Ernst Udet (one of the pilots in Richtofen's crack Red Baron fighter squadron in the First World War).

_____

[First published in *Ladies' Home Journal*, January 1944.]

Peter Shaw had got out of the cockpit and was leaning against the fuselage of his Avro, tugging at the chin strap of his helmet, when Juanita ran up. Several shades of East African dust were caked on his face, and his eyes were bloodshot. He was obviously dead tired, and there was justification for his impatience, which he presently displayed by breaking the strap and throwing the helmet on the ground. The act released his black hair, so that its smothered curls began to come alive in the wind. Dust or no dust, Peter was handsome by any standard, and Juanita had never been more aware of it; his features were too clean-cut to take harm from a bit of dirt, and his eyes too bold to suffer much from weariness or wind. His nose was straight as a blade and his lips were full. Beyond that, he had flat cheeks, which, at the moment, he was diligently scrubbing with the back of his hand.

Juanita came to him gently, and he grinned. It was a good grin, and he took her lightly in his arms and kissed her on the forehead, then held her a little away from him, appraising, with mock solemnity, her wide apart blue eyes, her shining, sun yellow hair.

"Hello, monkey," he said. "I'm glad I made it."

"Made what?" Juanita disengaged herself and looked at the Avro. She thought that it sagged a bit on the port side, but on the whole it looked pretty sound. She began to smile—and then the smile didn't come. Nothing came but a strange uneasiness, then a sharp awareness. She looked at the Avro again. Of course it sagged—a longeron was snapped like a piece of kindling struck with an axe—and the front seat, Michael's seat, was empty. She did not question Peter. She moved closer to him and put a hand on his arm and waited.

He glanced at his plane and swore softly. "My first forced landing," he explained. "The rains are on and I couldn't find

Marsabit. That was yesterday. It was getting dark and I had to come down in that darned lava desert about eighty miles north of the post." He handed her his flying map, marked clearly with a pencil dot. "Right there," he said. "Snapped a longeron getting down—and I'll never know how I managed to get off."

"And Michael?"

"He's all right. We don't have to worry." He spoke quickly but with weariness in his voice. "In the morning I saw I couldn't get the plane off with both of us in it—too much weight. We talked it over and Michael had to stay. It was the only way out. I left him what water there was and flew to Marsabit. They're sending a camel caravan out to get him." He managed a tired smile. "And that's the story. Now how about some tea?"

They had left the runway behind them and, walking arm in arm, had reached the little jungle of bougainvillea that guarded the veranda of her father's house.

Juanita was thoughtful. "That would be the Koroli Desert," she said, looking at the map again. "It's supposed to be one of the worst."

He nodded. "I can confirm it. It's terrible."

For a moment she was silent. She paused with her hand on the latch of the heavy *lamu* door that, like a portcullis, confronted the surrounding wilderness. She swept the wayward locks of blond hair away from her forehead as if meaning him to see the whole of her face as she turned it to him.

"Peter," she said hesitantly, almost with an air of apology, "I know you're worn out—and perhaps this is silly for me to say. I'm not used to this kind of thing yet—but shouldn't something more be done? Shouldn't you go back for Michael? If he's eighty miles north of Marsabit, camels won't reach him for days." She swept her hand toward the runway. "There's my plane; if you took the seats out to lighten it—or—" She paused again a little awkwardly, as if feeling that without the right to do it she was questioning his judgement. "It won't be dark for hours," she said. "I thought that perhaps—" Groping for words, she saw that Peter was looking down at her with surprise in his eyes, and she gave it up.

"Darling," he said firmly, "you never went in for heroics or hysterics before; you oughtn't to start now. Michael wouldn't expect me to chance my plane, or yours, on a fool's errand so long as there's a rescue party on the way. A good flier never risks the same accident twice. If you want to be good, remember that. You can't fly on your emotions." His voice was almost paternal. He was the teacher again, as she had known him in the cockpit—calm, sensible, sound. It was the quality that had given her such confidence in him. "It's the harebrained pilots that make people mistrust flying," he had often told her, "the hero boys full of daredevil nonsense from the last war, all anxious to have their necks broken in another one."

No, she conceded to herself, you couldn't fly on your emotions. Peter had confronted her with her own philosophy of sanity and realism, and she could not criticize him for it. If one man were lost in a desert, nothing could be gained by losing two. This must be—this was—truth. But still—

For a moment, she glanced back through her childhood memory, seeing herself and the redheaded Michael running forever, barefoot and happy, through the forest paths. She looked up at Peter and contrived a smile. "I'm sorry," she said. "He's such an old, old friend—and I can't help thinking."

"You needn't," said Peter. "The camels will find him."

She knew that he was right. But she had to tell herself that he was, had to check herself on the verge of stupidly insisting that he take her plane and go back after Michael. She had to close the doors of her mind against the sudden thought that in Peter's place, Michael would have gone back, would have insisted on going back.

A long time afterward, when it was midafternoon, she was still trying to shut that obstinately persisting thought out of her mind, the way the drawn curtains of her father's house were shutting out the equatorial sun, unchallenged master of this land even here in the foothills of Mount Kenya, whose crest was eternally studded with ice. Here in the long living room it was almost dark, and almost cool, and within the cedar walls there was an atmosphere—almost—of peace.

In a broad leather chair that leaned its back against a tier of bookshelves, she sat staring at the opposite wall without seeing it. What she saw was Peter's crippled plane as he maneuvered it, so cleverly and so carefully, from the runway and started for Nairobi. It had been gone for an hour, but the drone of it seemed scarcely dead in her ears.

She was being stupid, she told herself. Stupid and vain. Like the vain, stupid women who demanded that their men be heroes, because the men they read about and saw in films and perhaps dreamed about were always heroes. The kind of heroes who got themselves cut to ribbons or blown to bits for no better reason than to let some woman salve her silly ego with the thought, "He did it for me!"

She ought to be rejoicing that Peter wasn't that kind of hero. That he'd done the sensible, the right things, the things that were as wise and safe for Michael as for Peter himself. The surest way of getting Michael out of that desert alive had been to leave him there, with water, to make for Marsabit and send those camels out to bring him back. The camels were certain to do it. In a little time, perhaps in only a few hours, the word would come that all was well, and she would be glad that she'd been sensible, too, as sensible as Peter, and left a man's problem for men to cope with.

But she stirred in her chair, and pushed her hair back from her forehead with a quick, almost fretful gesture, as if her hand could brush away the question that was in her mind. She did not want to think. Beyond everything she did not want to think. But she did not know why this was so.

She closed her eyes and held them closed while Ismail, the Somali houseboy, entered the room on noiseless feet and performed his special rite. Every afternoon at just this hour he lit the incense. It was incense brought from Aden, near the Red Sea, and, as a Somali, he had a reverence for it. It was nostalgia made sweet, and its fragrance, blended of myrrh and frankincense, was as much a part of the Martin house as Ismail himself.

Perhaps it was the act itself, performed in silence except for the hypnotic rustle of Ismail's *khansa*, that made Juanita sleep. Certainly she had not intended to. She sat still in the deep chair and nodded like a drowsy child, a troubled child, and when she awoke—not with a start, but gently—her eyes were on the little iron brazier where the incense burned. As she watched the blue smoke, dreamily at first, it seemed to her that it rose erratically. Then, in the half-light of the curtained room, it seemed to make a kind of pattern, dimly remembered but familiar.

North from Marsabit toward the Kenya-Ethiopia border, the Koroli Desert spreads with the aimlessness of all deserts, admitting no boundary save the sky. But to the practiced eye, to the desert-born, the Koroli Desert is clearly marked with the symbols of its special character. It is no sea of yellow sand lapping at the shores of an occasional oasis; it is a crowded desert, dry as bleaching bones, but furnished, as few deserts are, with countless monstrous black lava shapes, sculptured and bequeathed by some cataclysm-minded god, aeons ago. The dismal monuments rise at every hand, and a man among them is to himself, and to them, without existence; he is better than lost. His being is without significance. If he has water, he can delude himself while it lasts. If he has hope, he can sing; if he has courage, he can work—it hurries time.

Michael was hurrying time. He both worked and sang. Fairly tall, his body had a wiry, whiplike quality; the distinguishing feature of his face was its simplicity. A lean face, starred with freckles, surmounted by a mop of reddish hair and lighted with blue eyes, it obviously had never concealed a secret and masked few, if any, doubts. It was open and unperturbed.

He wore the uniform of an officer of the King's Africa Rifles: khaki shorts, a tunic of the same stuff, bearing mathematically spaced pockets, a military helmet. A metal water bottle dangled from a strap hung over his shoulder and now and then swung in wide arcs as he strained and sweated against a black rock and dragged it from the clearing he had planned. He was making a runway for an airplane, and the job was plainly impossible. He sang gaily—but with no tone and no respect for melody—the chorus of Schubert's melancholy "Serenade," and the impassioned words wandered without goal or audience through the labyrinth of rock.

He had cleared a space perhaps twenty feet wide and fifty feet long—scarcely enough room, he thought, in which to toss a cat, much less swing it. But it didn't matter. There would probably be no plane anyway, but the job kept him occupied while he waited for the camels.

"Under my window, deep in the shadows"—he sang loudly, apparently unaware that, since there were no shadows anywhere within the scope of his sight, the words were mildly ironic—"sings the nightingale."

He paused there, unsure of the verse, indifferent to the fact that the only bird within view was a vulture, mute, intent, ploughing the sky back and forth on hopeful wings. Having paused in his singing, he reproached himself for having sung at all. It made his throat dry. He reached down for the water bottle at his hip, held it to his ear and shook it. This morning it had gurgled; now it only tinkled. He wanted to drink, but rejected the impulse, thinking of tomorrow.

According to his watch, it was an hour past noon. He had a handful of dates wrapped in a handkerchief. He ate four of them and put the little bundle that remained into the pocket of his shirt. He was hungry and his mouth seemed dry as the sand he waded in, but he felt that he was getting used to the heat. It was everywhere, coming up from the earth, radiating from the lava boulders, pouring even from his body so that, to himself, he seemed no longer alien to the desert, but a part of it.

He remembered that, in theory, a man without sufficient water was supposed to die after forty-eight hours of such exposure, but he counted this as nonsense. The brief spasms of dizziness that were beginning to plague him as he worked were, he decided, due to fatigue; he had moved a lot of rock; all that he needed was to rest.

He closed his eyes and crouched against a shaft of rock that jutted from the sand. He was breathing with some effort, but that would soon pass. He groped in a pocket and brought out a square of shining paper. It was a print of a careless snapshot taken some years ago as Juanita Martin and he had stood hand in hand over the body of a marauding leopard they had trapped together. It had been their first great adventure. He did not dwell upon it, but when he returned it to his pocket, the urge to sing had left him. Still, he did not allow himself a maudlin sigh; it was pointless to wish.

For a long time now he had discounted himself as a romantic figure, and it seemed to him that all the girls he had ever known had upheld him in this judgement. He was irrevocably the constant friend, the old dependable—the good sound wine that never sparkled.

He shook his water bottle again, ruled temptation down, and began to labor over a rock. It was heavy, but he pried it from its hollow and lifted it with both arms, holding it against his body. He struggled toward the edge of his tiny clearing, sinking to his ankles in the sand, shaking his head against the salt sweat that blinded his eyes.

He could not have seen the almost buried blade of lava that ran across his path, for he stumbled over it with the rock in his arms, and went down swearing mildly at his clumsiness. He was not hurt. Not even his fingers were hurt; the fall was gentle, and it was not until he stood up again and began automatically to dust his clothes that he saw that his water bottle had burst open under the impact of the rock and had poured its contents on the sand. He did not reach for it, nor make any move. He stood swaying a little with the heat of the desert crowding him, watching the dark spot the cupful of water had made at his feet. Finally he took one of the two cigarettes that were left to him and lit it and drew the smoke in deeply.

Under my window, deep in the shadows—aimlessly the words wandered through his mind, but did not reach his lips. The smoke from his cigarette rose from his hand straight to the sky like a rope at a magician's bidding. He observed it idly, feeling the dizziness again, and closed his eyes until it had passed.

Well, he thought, here it was—the classic desert tragedy, a stranded man without water. It was so hackneyed, so melodramatic a situation as to be almost shameful. At the thought of it he tried to smile, but he knew that the effort was false. He knew that it was the sun and not fatigue that was draining the strength from his legs and his arms and making his vision more blurred, moment by moment. He had known it for hours.

Now it came again—the weakness that ran through his body like a fever and, like a fever, left him trembling and yearning to let himself fall upon the sand and stay there, forgetting everything. But once more he waited until it had gone, steadying himself, staring at his burning cigarette as if sanity—and even hope—were to be found only in the contemplation of the little rod of grey smoke that tapered toward the sun.

Smoke. Closing his eyes, he remembered a game they used to play—Juanita and he—a game with smoke. It had been simple. You built a fire somewhere on the veld, not too far from the farm, and you kept yourself hidden. Then with your hat, or with a sheaf of grass, you broke the smoke into puffs and made signals like the natives. Three short puffs and a long one, for instance, always meant "Come quickly, the fort is falling." It had been fun to make the signal and see how long it took for your most special friend to find you and arrive, breathless, with a handful of stone or a *Wandorobo* bow and arrow for your support against the enemy.

Three short puffs and a long one. Almost dreamily, with half a smile on his lips, Michael Cole knelt in the sand and lighted a scrap of paper from his pocket. Crawling on his knees, he collected bits of desert grass and threw them on the feeble flame. He found the stems of dry thorns and added them to it one by one like a miser paying pennies. He would

have searched farther had he found the strength to move another step, but, like the water in the broken bottle, the
strength had run out of him.

When the flame had grown to the size of a small bush, he
pulled his battered hat from his head, and time after time, until
he began to fall into what he supposed was sleep, he sent the
smoke upward in three short puffs and then a long one, while
there was willingness in his arms, the childish message.

Desert grass and thorns are not long-burning. For perhaps
five minutes the little fire smoldered, and when it went out he
was unconscious of it. He lay with his red hair in the sand,
breathing slowly while his sole companion, the vulture overhead, swung nearer on rigid wings.

Juanita got to her feet and stood for a moment, trembling.
She walked over to the brazier and watched it closely. The
smoke from the incense rose in an unbroken band of blue.

"It was a dream," she said. "It couldn't have been a signal.
Not for me."

She went to the window and opened the curtains on the
empty sky. She thought of her meagre sixty hours of flying
time, her uncertain skill with compass and calculator, her constant concern with the vastness of the land. She thought of Peter's face, looking the way it would look at her if he knew
about the futile, senseless thing she wanted to do, the utterly
unreasonable reason why she wanted to do it.

"He's right," she said. "I couldn't—"

But she took the map that Peter had left with her and held
it tightly in her hand. She looked at her watch. She took her
flying goggles from a drawer in the table. Peter's face was still
watching her. She answered what it was saying.

"I know," she said. "I'll never find him."

Sleep had gone from her eyes and they were shining

strangely. She ran through the house and out along the path to the runway that had been, when she and Michael were children, a field of grass to others, but to them a hundred things: a sea, a jungle, a city with gleaming streets, an undiscovered world—a desert.

"The fort is falling," she murmured as she ran, "the fort is falling!"

From the air the Koroli Desert seems especially designed to conceal a stranded man. In the midst of a hundred thousand lava rocks, some tall as a man, some prone like resting human figures, some kneeling like men at prayer or men digging for water—where is the man himself? He is everywhere and so does not exist at all.

After hours at the controls of her Gypsy Moth, Juanita Martin knew, if she had not known it before, how complete despair could be. Cautiously, she had clung to her course, anxiously she had pored over Peter's map in the painful knowledge that figures, the cold needle of the compass, the comfortless chart across her knees were, in her hands, the fallible links between herself and Michael. Yet nowhere, she assured herself, had she gone wrong.

There, to the west, neither like silver nor like blue nor even shining, but dull as rust and sullen in the sun, sprawled Lake Rudolf. Before her, under the belly of the plane, beyond her, behind her and to the east there was the desert. Had it not spread in all directions past the limit of sight, it might have been the ruins of an ancient city burned to earth, the fallen columns of its buildings in a charred jumble, its symmetry vanished with age. Disconsolately she realized that a single man lost here might be lost forever, and in the realization she admitted that if Peter's reason had seemed to her without sympathy, it had still been reason. Here, at the prompting of a childhood memory—a wisp of smoke—she flew under the guidance of little else but impulse on an impossible errand.

She could still turn back. The hot swift wind that invaded the open cockpit scorched her cheeks. For better vision she had pushed her goggles from her eyes, and they wept from the sting and the glare. But these were physical discomforts, far less important than the dawning knowledge that she was afraid.

She was caught between two fears. With little more than an hour of daylight left, she might turn back to Marsabit before dark, and the fear that lack of courage might force her to do it was no less than the fear that nightfall might find her still above the hostile land—and without fuel.

Again and again she circled over what, according to her calculations, would be the dot that Peter had indicated on his map. Nowhere was there any sign of life. Inscrutable and silent, the desert waited beneath her wings, and in the end she turned.

She could not fly forever staring with blinded eyes on an unvarying scene that yielded her nothing. For what, to her, was time without end, she had hung like this—on hope and on those feeble wings—and there was nothing. Sick in her heart, she pressed the rudder bar and mapped her course to Marsabit, and counted herself a fool. She had proven nothing save that Peter had, after all, been right.

Unreasonably she let frustration turn to anger, and anger to imprudence. She pushed the throttle, accelerating the little plane almost beyond its limit of speed, and roared toward Marsabit. Minutes and miles disappeared behind her, hand in hand, and the voice of the Gypsy Moth jeered of failure, and the tears in her eyes were not from wind alone.

When she saw the camel caravan stirring the dust in lazy

wisps from the desert, she was halfway to Marsabit and the sun lay low and red upon the farthest dunes. Inexperienced though she was, it did not take her more than a moment to compute that the caravan was off its course, not by much, but by enough to miss its goal by several miles.

She did not hesitate. If she had thought, she would not have turned back again, but she did not allow herself to think. She banked the plane in a wide, clear arc and flew once more toward the desert in what was left of the day's last light. She flew low in a kind of urgent despair, swinging the little craft back and forth not five hundred feet above the ground, ignoring her dwindling supply of fuel, handling the controls with careless intimacy born not of skill, but of bitterness and desperation.

Now she began to wonder if she had not been committed to this search, not just from the moment Peter had flown to Nairobi, but long before, years before, perhaps. Vague questions that had never confronted her began to rise in discomforting shapes to cloud her vision. She began to speculate on her love for Peter, on its whirlwind beginning at the dance at the Muthaiga Club in Nairobi, a beginning that had been without question, perhaps even without understanding. She could not be sure—but now, each time she envisioned Peter's appealing, masculine figure, his carefree manner, his dark eyes so often lighted with gaiety, the slight unprepossessing presence of Michael Cole was in the vision, too, until both men were confused and mingled in her memory.

Impatiently, she banished thought and tried to concentrate on the task at hand. She had not enough fuel with which to return to Marsabit, and dusk was not far off. Shadows of rock had begun to spread themselves on the desert like an army of men preparing for sleep, but there was no man among them. Nor would there be, she decided. She had failed miserably in a wild, quixotic quest. More—as a pilot she was guilty of the ultimate sin: she had allowed herself no safety, no retreat.

The drone of the plane and the coming of night and the hopelessness made her want to sleep, as if sleep could drug discouragement and make fear numb. At a thousand feet she leveled the craft and held it level, flying north. Below her the desert was cooling; the tone and feel of the wind in the wires and on the wings were changed. The light was failing. And it seemed to come not from the sky in which she flew, but from the earth, making the sand translucent and the black rocks gleam. Once more she swung the plane east and then south.

She was almost incapable of thought or action when she saw below her the grooves that the wheels of a plane had left, deep and evenly spaced in the shifting sand. By morning, perhaps within another hour, the night wind would have erased the sign.

Without thought she began to spiral earthward, without even wondering whether she was capable of side-slipping deftly enough to make the almost impossible landing. Cautiously, boldly, as if she had done it a thousand times, she pushed the stick to the left and put pressure on the right rudder bar and then reversed the action, tipping the plane from side to side, spilling the air from its wings until it began to fall like a wounded hawk, until the earth came up like darkness and struck the craft and the sound of tearing wires and fabric and snapping wood burst in her ears and she felt her body plunge against the belt that held her in the cockpit, and consciousness left her.

When she recovered consciousness the sun had gone and massive shadows stalked the desert. She was dazed and her legs were numb but there was no pain, no blood. She was not hurt, but she saw that her plane had lost a wing against a jutting rock. It would not fly from this place. She unfastened the safety belt and climbed down and stared about her. There was neither movement nor breath of life.

She shouted, but there was no answer. She groped in the plane and got a water bottle, then a flashlight, and swung its hard, white beam from rock to dune and from dune to rock, and there was nothing.

She moved away from the plane into the forest of shapeless masses, stumbling as she walked, calling Michael's name and receiving, in turn, an echo. Despair began to fill her heart and would have filled it, but the light fell upon a smudge of ash at her feet, black ash, pitifully small, and dead, but hoarded like a wealth of gold dust in a hand-scooped hollow. A small dead fire. With a scorched, battered hat beside it. She followed the tracks Michael had made with his dragging feet until she found him, not fifty feet beyond, his red hair seemingly no longer red, but dimmed by the color of the sand he lay in, the skin of his face scorched and peeling, his eyes closed.

She dropped her light and lifted his head from the sand and brought the water to his clenched lips and poured it on them and forced it into his mouth. After a long, long time he stirred and his eyes looked up into hers. Still uncertain, he lifted a hand, touched her cheek.

"How did you know?" His voice was a child's voice, trailing across the edge of sleep.

She seemed to hear, but very far away, Peter's patient, sensible voice reminding her that you couldn't fly on your emotions. Or live by them. She didn't attempt to answer Michael except by the pressure of her heart against his cradled head. She had always known, she thought now, that her heart would find its way to Michael.

The Transformation

The tall, rough-handed, blunt John Craig in this story could well be based on Beryl's first husband, Jock Purves. Beryl was sixteen when she married Jock, a former Scottish International Rugby Football player, twice her age. He was a neighbor of Beryl's father, and the scene where the storyteller meets John has a ring of reality about it. "I used to ride through a corner of his pastures, and I found him there one morning stretching wire on fence posts. . . ." Beryl's marriage to Jock lasted less than two years and it is tempting to think that John's clumsy yet confident ability on his farm, and his inability to relate emotionally to the needs of the sensitive Anne, might cast some light on Beryl's own situation.

Jock eventually returned to London where he became a sports journalist for The Times. Perhaps this struck Beryl as just as unlikely an occurrence as the profession provided for John Craig at the end of this story.

I first saw him at a gunsmith's shop in Nairobi. He was a huge man, young—twenty-six, perhaps—and he knew nothing of guns, nor did he want to. He was new to Kenya, but not to farming, and he had bought a tract of uncleared land up near the Mau forest, where leopards had of course begun to prey

[First published in *Ladies' Home Journal*, January 1946.]

upon his livestock. He needed a rifle, he explained to the clerk, and as he examined three or four, I saw that he handled them without respect or appreciation. His hands were strong and insensitive, and he would jerk open the breech of a finely made weapon as if it were a rusted piece of machinery. In the end he chose a light Springfield of excellent design and walked away holding it as if it were an axe.

The clerk shook his head and looked at me. "He'll prop windows open with it," he said, "and let the barrel rust."

"I suppose so," I said. I didn't care whether or not he split wood with it, but I remembered the way he used his hands.

It proved to be the way he used everything. As we learned more of him we saw that his mind was as harsh as his touch. He was not cruel, but there was no sentiment in him that one could see, nor much curiosity except about material things that he could turn to his needs. What he did not understand he shrugged away. But he worked wonders with what he knew.

In very little time he cleared a hundred acres of his farm, blasting the stumps of massive trees, dragging boulders with teams of oxen, and finally gouging the soil in precise and parallel furrows—for he did not seem to plough the land, but to harass it with a kind of anxious fury until it bore. He had no talent for the earth and pretended none, but he knew it chemically and made it yield.

His house was built in a matter of weeks. It stood high and alone on the rim of the Rongai Valley—a dark intrusion on the gentle skyline. It was clean and square and bleak. Nothing could get into it that he did not want to get in, and among those things was cheer as other people knew it. Still, as a house, it was beyond criticism. It was solid, tight—a flawless shelter—and when the last nail had been sunk into its cedar planking, John Craig decided to marry.

It was not an extraordinary decision except that it was so deliberately made and that, to the surprise of everyone, he set his mind on the one girl who was almost beyond his reach and certainly beyond his understanding. She was Anne Barton, whom Craig had met not more than twice, and who was in any case in love with another man, Larry Abbot, an independent pilot, the possessor of countless friends, but with not a shilling to his name.

Everyone knew about Anne and Larry; they seemed almost of a single identity, though for all of that it was a strange relationship. For three years their eventual marriage had been taken for granted, but it remained "eventual"; it had never happened, simply because Larry remained too improvident to make it happen. Yet Larry and Anne were inseparable, and his adoration of her must have been as plain to John Craig as it was to everyone; still it had no effect on him. He was ready to marry and Anne Barton was the girl he wanted.

He went to Anne and made his fantastic proposal with such bluntness as can come only from a man of massive ego, and he was turned away with more grace, but with equal bluntness.

Anne Barton was essentially feminine, essentially gentle, and she had more wisdom at twenty-two, I think, than is commonly combined with beauty. She was a slender girl with chestnut hair that shone above deep eyes with a curious light in them. Perhaps they were sad eyes—they were at least musing—but she had a wealth of laughter nonetheless, laughter hoarded, as it were, against the moment and the friend. She lived alone in Nairobi, working as a secretary in order to live, but for the love of the world she worked at being a sculptress; and while she had never had formal training in this, her hands could and did communicate to clay the strange intensity that was always in her eyes.

Of course she turned John Craig away, but not with anger or out of any affectation of outraged pride. She told him that he ought to see more of women—of other women.

"It's not enough just to be a man," she said, "even a strong and competent man. Women are not beggars, John. They don't have to take what's offered them. They choose, and the qualities they want are not what you think them to be. It's strange you haven't learned that. But one day you will."

He went away then, a giant of a man, stung deeply, yet proud and unbelieving because he could not believe in anything except himself—and I cannot say that he ever changed in that. And yet because of what happened a little later, during his inevitable quarrel with Larry Abbot, I am not sure, nor will I ever be.

I was myself a free-lance pilot in those days, and since Larry had taught me much of what I knew about flying, we saw each other almost daily at the Nairobi airport. His passion for the work was so intense that he had no room in his head or heart for the business of it. He made a living with his two planes, but it was a bare living when in East Africa at that time he might have made a small fortune. He was a slender man—about twenty-four then—with nothing arresting about him except searching grey eyes, fine hands, and a smile that he seemed to reserve for small tragedy. Everything held a meaning for him, and he would spend hours in his plane alone and often by night because, as he once said, he was fascinated by "the furnishings of darkness."

All in all, he was as different from John Craig as a plane is different from a plough, and it was this difference, among other things, that made it seem inevitable that he and Anne must one day marry. And yet, though he was deeply in love with her, he was equally in love with solitude and Anne was afraid of that. Very often he would slide into the cockpit of his plane, wave a hand, and take off, to be gone for days on a profitless flight. He would fly into Tanganyika, or Abyssinia, or perhaps into the Belgian Congo, and when he came back, strangely refreshed, he would go to Anne, finding her in her tiny studio of half-born figures of clay, and they would talk for hours and laugh together—and make dreams that never came true. He offered her everything of the spirit, and she returned in kind and seemed happy. Yet, being a woman, she could want fulfillment of a kind he did not understand, and his repeated plea for marriage was turned back again and again because she believed that he thought of it too lightly—not as the profound and deep responsibility she wanted it to be. This was the constant hurt to him, so it was natural that, when word of Craig's heavy-handed proposal to Anne reached Larry's ears, he was shocked and angered—shocked by what seemed to him the boorishness of it, and angered because it had never occurred to him that, marriage or not, Anne was not wholly his own.

"Craig may not know any better," Larry said to me, "but it's no excuse! How can you go to a woman you scarcely know and say, 'Look, I've got a farm and a new house and some cows, and now I want you for a wife'? What kind of man will do that?"

We were standing by the hangar at the airport, waiting for the low clouds to rise from the runway. Larry's rusty hair was tangled by the antics of a feeble morning breeze, his flying clothes—shirt, slacks, and sneakers—were crumpled, but somehow neat. He swung his goggles from his forefinger in a little nervous arc.

"What kind of man?" he demanded again.

I didn't answer at once. I knew what kind of man, but I also knew about Larry—about his gentle irresponsibility, the ease with which he could detach himself from practical matters. It seemed to me that he was half a man, the sensitive, generous, and forever-undecided half, while John Craig was the other half—muscle, mind, and ego. Neither man was complete. Each, I thought, lacked the virtues of the other, and because of that their mutual contempt in the end must congeal into hard constructive hatred, though at that time they barely knew each other by sight.

"John Craig is not a subtle man," I said. "But he meant no insult to Anne. He just doesn't understand gentleness or tact."

"Or much else," said Larry, "except his farm and his boorish vanity. What he can't bend, he wants to break. But there are ways of curing that."

He shrugged then and went into the hangar, and I went toward my own plane, which was already on the runway.

My father's farm and John Craig's were neighboring, and I would fly up from Nairobi on weekends or when the business of transporting mail and hunters into the hinterland slacked off a bit. On those occasions I would sometimes see John working in his fields or with his cattle. He was unchanging, outwardly content in his loneliness—tall, rough-handed, blunt. Somehow he gave the impression of a man cut off from the society of other men by the mere fact that he did not know their language of casual talk and quick laughter, and could not learn it.

I used to ride through a corner of his pastures, and I found him there one morning stretching wire on fence posts. His tools were a small bar with a claw in it and a hammer. He could catch the wire in the claw, then draw it taut against the post, and staple it. Twice while I watched he broke the heavy strands as if they were clotheslines, because when his strength began to pour through his massive arms, he seemed unable to check it. Of course, when he was finished his fence was tighter than anyone else's.

When the work was done, and not until then, he looked up and nodded. In the bright Kenya sun his large tanned face was at once striking and a little pathetic. He wiped sweat from his jaws and his neck and stood waiting for my opinion of his place. I could see the question in his eyes. They were the eyes of an arrogant child demanding praise. But at the same time they were guarded and sharp with challenge.

We were on a rise of ground, and from my saddle I could look over his farm. It was finished. It was so complete, so precisely arranged that it might have been a painting by a commercial draftsman. It was too orderly, and I felt that even the cattle had taken their places in the various fields out of deference to the whole design.

"What do you think of it?" he said.

"You've made a fine thing of it. It's like a blueprint—exactly like a blueprint."

The comparison pleased him. He looked proudly at what he had built. Then at once he turned on me in frowning petulance.

"Good," he said, "good! Then tell me this. You've lived here all your life, and you know Anne Barton. If my farm is what you say it is—is there any reason why she shouldn't want to live on it?"

Perhaps a Breton peasant might have asked that question— some man to whom a woman was no more than a practical complement to his cow barns, his henhouse, and his kitchen. But Craig was no peasant.

"There's nothing wrong with your farm," I said. "But women don't marry farms. Not Anne, at least, and it's time you knew it."

He only shrugged. "She can't live on dreams," he said, "or on air—especially with a man who spends most of his time in the middle of one or the other." It was an obvious reference to Larry, and it was all the sharper for the truth that was in it. But more than that there was disdain in it, and contempt.

"It's true that Larry is no farmer," I said. "He'd be no good at it. But then, you're no flier—and probably if you tried you would be no good at that."

He straightened immediately and cocked his head a little to one side, as if he couldn't believe what I had said, and I knew that I had blundered. He was no man to admit inferiority in anything, and now he felt challenged, though indirectly, by a man he instinctively and jealously hated.

"A plane is a machine, isn't it?" he said.

I nodded. "A plane is a machine." It would have been futile, I thought, to point out that such planes as we then flew were something more than just machines—and something less. They were fledgling things of wood and wire and cloth. More often than not they were equipped with engines too powerful for their fragile frames, or—as in Larry's Klemm—with engines so feeble as almost to require of the pilot the sensitive touch of a pianist to keep them in harmony with the weather and the wind.

And yet John Craig was saying, "I know machines. I can handle machines, though I never thought it much of a way to test a man. Still, it seems the idea appeals to women—men in ships, men in planes, men with their feet off the ground. Well, if that's what's wanted, it's easy enough. I'll fly."

It seemed at the moment no more than a boast born out of simple masculine pride. It was as if he had said, "I know women. I can handle women!"

I reined my horse toward my father's farm. Glancing back, I

saw that Craig had undertaken to split a log of cedar for his fence. He did not do it patiently by the use of a wedge and hammer, but by wrathful, even wild, blows of his enormous axe; and somehow that picture came into my mind at once, when two days later, to the astonishment of both Larry and myself, Craig strode across the Nairobi airport and demanded that Larry teach him to fly.

It was a strange and disquieting moment. Nurtured by silence, the enmity of each toward the other had grown and taken the formless and unreasonable shape of all things that thrive without light. There was no understanding, not even enough for anger.

They looked at each other for a moment: Larry, slender, motionless, outwardly at ease, smiling his bittersweet smile; and Craig, big, but bigger still with arrogance, framed in the hangar door. Craig held a scrap of newspaper in his hand. It was the small advertisement Larry had run for months, not really to increase his income but to please some insistent friend who sold such ads. There it was, in John Craig's hand, and he was saying:

"You're Abbot, aren't you? Well, as you know, I'm John Craig, and I want to fly. You can show me the tricks."

All the condescension in the world was in his voice—all the patronizing inflection of the sturdy realist addressing the dreamer. And the dreamer might easily have laughed him away. It was what I hoped for, expected, I think. But there were more subtle shades to Larry's nature. I looked at his face and saw that he was still smiling his dry, mirthless smile. His grey eyes, aglow with irony, were very steady and very thoughtful. He knew the challenge for what it was. He shifted his glance from Craig's face to Craig's massive hands that were like great, insensitive clamps. Then he looked with meaning at the fragile little plane already shivering on the runway under the morning wind. The plane was sky blue, and on its fuselage was neatly painted the name: *ANNE*. He turned to me and nodded toward the scrap of newsprint in John Craig's hand.

"The power of the printed word," he said, smiling his sardonic smile, "it brings all things to all men. All right, Craig, we fly."

They took off at once: Larry at the controls, with more than a hint of disdain in his manner; Craig in the rear cockpit, his shoulders squared in arrogance. And when at last the little craft was airborne, droning its reproach against the sky, I could not help thinking that no smaller world could be contrived for two men so hateful of each other. But in an instant they were gone, and with time and distance closed behind them I went about my own work, servicing my plane for a routine flight to Mombasa.

What happened after that is difficult to tell, because part of the story is lost.

I returned just before dark, landing my Avian on the rough plot we called an airport, and I saw then that Larry Abbot and John Craig had not come back. There was no word, nor any sign of them, but I was not immediately worried. I saw to it that flares were lighted on the edges of the runway, and then I went into Nairobi, telling myself that they would come in by night.

But they did not come in that night, nor the next night, nor the night after that, and there was no message. There was nothing.

On the second day I went to Anne and told her what had happened, and I saw at once that she was afraid for Larry—for both of them. She did not hate John Craig, but she feared the fury of his jealousy and strength. And she knew Larry; she knew his tenacity, his determination to humiliate the big man. It was like a knife against a bludgeon.

"It's not just a legend," she said, "that this country does strange things to men. They get drunk on the bigness of it. They throw restraint away, and reason goes with it. They should not be together in that plane!"

She was not given to hysteria, but she was deeply concerned. I watched her pace her tiny, cluttered workshop, a slender, vital, yet very feminine girl. Almost a child, I thought, and it came to me that she was out of place among her pedestals and lumps of clay. It was make-believe, and I suddenly knew why, because I remembered that once she had stood with a clay figure that she had made, and had looked at it heavy in her hand, and then had said, "I wish it were a child— my child." It was a thing that Larry could never understand because it would have meant the sacrifice of his constant flirtation with unreality. It would have meant responsibility, regularity, worry—the coarser threads that go into the weaving of happiness. Nor could John Craig have understood it.

I stood up and moved toward the door. "I'll take off in the morning," I said, "toward Marsabit. They went north."

We had no radios then; nor any shortwave station in East Africa, for that matter. When a plane vanished, you did the simple thing: you looked for it, hoping that if it had force-landed, it had found some better place than the vast Mau forest, the slopes of Kilimanjaro, or the steaming elephant country to the south. I knew all the hopes. I had searched before for lost planes—and found a few.

But I did not find this one. No one ever did, though there were countless parties organized. And then, after eleven interminable days and nights, we learned by messenger that two men had crawled one morning from the rim of the Koroli Desert to the shelter of an Indian trader's camp. They were John Craig and Larry Abbot, of course—and they were nearly dead.

Men have been lost and found before—many in Africa, some in the Koroli Desert, a place of monstrous rocks burning in a sea of sand—and most times such men have a story to tell, and they tell it. These men did not. A few natives and settlers remembered seeing the plane in broad daylight and clear weather. Some said its course was erratic, its control unstable. Others said it flew straight for the desert, willfully guided there. Perhaps it does not matter, and perhaps the story of John Craig's and Larry Abbot's eleven days and nights in that prison of rock and sand does not matter either, since neither man would ever speak of it.

And yet, one wonders. I, at least, am haunted now and then by the patchwork story of the Indian trader who nursed them, in his way, for many hours, and who seemed, when I spoke to him long afterward, an incurious man, but one of precise memory. He was a Sikh, and I remember his great turban of dirty cloth that seemed so white against his earthy skin, so fresh above his tired eyes.

"I saw them at dawn, memsahib," he said, "not men to the eye, but mounds of flesh for jackals. Yet they breathed, and the jackal does not touch what breathes, memsahib. I brought them here."

His trader's shack—his *duka*—was four walls of mud and daub, his merchandise the cherished luxuries and tinsel of a dozen native tribes. The men had crawled, he said, part way, and he had helped and guided them. They needed water and he had given that, and bathed their lips and burning eyes until they slept.

"Then they were not hurt," I asked, "except by the sun?"

He looked at the sun, as if to question it, and then he looked at me. "The sun, memsahib, may sometimes choke a man, but it leaves no mark upon his throat."

I hesitated, but he would not be hurried. "Which man?" I finally asked.

The old Sikh shrugged. He was explicit. "The mark of the big one was on the throat of the other. A strong mark, memsahib—a death mark—but the fingers of the big one's hand were broken." He smiled musingly. "A little man can break a little bone," he said.

"I see," I told him and nodded.

So it had come to that. I wondered what had given impetus to that silent, lonely struggle in the sand. Two men—both strong, but one immense—shuffling, swaying, groping, each for the other's life. A knife against a bludgeon—the quick, sharp cleverness of Larry, the knotted muscles of Craig.

"And after that?" I turned again to the Sikh.

"There was blood on both," he said. "And this, memsahib, was a strange thing to my eye—that when I found them, the wounds of each were wrapped, with care, in the clothing of the other!"

I got no more from him, and never will; it was all he knew. But when I left, he handed me a crumpled note in Larry's writing—a note the Sikh had picked up from the floor where Craig had lain.

"I cannot read, memsahib. Does this have meaning?"

To me it had. It was the kind of note that was exchanged between the cockpits when the roar of the engine was too loud for speech. I read it slowly.

"Better admit you can't fly, Craig—just yet, and maybe

never. You're over the Koroli, and in trouble. I can take over, and I will—when you ask it. Give your pride a breather. Live and learn."

That was it—Larry, smiling still, and still sardonic, watched the little plane under Craig's thick-handed guidance plunge and tremble over the hot, swift currents of the desert. And there was Craig, out of control, trampling the rudder bar, clutching the stick as if it were his heavy axe—and swearing to God that he would see them crash on the Koroli sand before he asked for help. And they had crashed because each must test the mettle of the other like sabres crossed in battle. Steel against steel. Pride against pride. Male against male.

And yet, in the end, as the old Sikh said: "The wounds of each were wrapped, with care, in the clothing of the other!"

Enemies—comrades for a while—but they did not become friends. It would be easier to say that whatever they had endured had bound them together and made them friends, but it wasn't so. They never spoke again—and yet they were not the same again. It was as if two disparate elements had been somehow ground in a crucible until each took essence from the other.

A little later Anne and Larry were married, and after that Anne had the child she wanted, and a certain crispness crept slowly into Larry's manner and into his life—an alertness, a sense of direction. He planned air routes and turned his dreams into money. He bought equipment and was as hard as iron in the bargaining. He gained stature, and friends who knew him for his bittersweet smile and his careless ways admired him later for what they called his "drive." Success came to him, and a woman's happiness to Anne.

Craig saw her once to say good-bye. His arrogance had strangely crumbled, and with it his farm. It became in time no longer the draftsman's drawing, but a warm and happily disordered place of foraging livestock and uneven fields. At last he sold it and wandered out of Africa—disconsolately, I suppose—but I had word of him.

Years later a friend from England said to me, "Do you remember Craig?" and again I saw the big man as he had once stood with his great angry axe, splitting a tree as if he were Vulcan forging armor for the gods.

"I remember Craig," I said.

"He's a doctor now," my friend said, "a surgeon in a children's clinic of the London slums."

I looked at him closely, and then I said the only thing that I could say—the only thing that would come to my mind: "A doctor? A surgeon? With those enormous hands?"

My friend nodded, smiling a little. "Yes," he said, "with those enormous hands."

PART FOUR

The Quitter

"The Quitter" was the last story Beryl wrote. It was written at the Santa Barbara cottage set high in a wooded canyon that had once been the romantic hideaway of her friends Leopold Stokowski and Greta Garbo.

It was an unhappy time for Beryl and for Raoul. He had begun to drink heavily and put on weight. The little writing Raoul produced would not sell, and the couple had severe financial difficulties. The problems were not one-sided. Beryl was scornful of failure and treated Raoul badly. Her frequent extramarital relationships further contributed to the breakdown of the union, and their rows became frequent and violent.

Beryl evidently wrote this story herself—probably out of financial desperation—but when she presented it to Raoul for editing (prior to its submission to a publisher), he was still sulking after a violent disagreement. He refused to help and Beryl was deeply upset. She submitted the unedited manuscript, but it was rejected. Consequently she turned to an old friend— the writer Stuart Cloete—for help. Cloete edited the story, which was later accepted for publication. It is perhaps the change in editor that accounts for the distinctive style of this story.

All the story's ingredients are those of Beryl's own life: the problems of a trainer, the thrill and apprehension of racing; the despair of a woman facing financial ruin; the greatness of a horse. Beryl was always at her best

[First published in *Cosmopolitan*, June 1946.]

*when writing about horses. She understood horses in a very special way
and, more than any man, not even excluding her beloved father, they were
the real love of her life.*

*"The Quitter" may have been the last thing that Beryl ever wrote,
though some years ago there was a manuscript of an unfinished novel—
believed to be the novel that she was working on jointly with Raoul, when
she visited Kenya and Somalia in 1947, a year after this story was written—among the papers at Beryl's cottage in Nairobi. That manuscript
disappeared some time after 1983.*

Mat Dixon's lips were unmoving. He looked at the girl
through grey, reluctant eyes that gave no answer. His hands
were folded on the desk, where he kept them in a single hard-
ened fist as if they held the word she wanted. English sunlight
lay in the room in golden ribbons, giving glow to things not
meant to glow, but it lent no warmth to the girl's precisely
sculptured face.

Sunlight on marble, Mat Dixon thought. He watched her
move in her chair, not petulantly, but with a kind of regal impatience, as she always moved when she asked for the impossible and intended to get it. Perhaps beauty alone did that to
some women, Dixon thought. It gave them arrogance the way
great strength gives arrogance to certain men.

"Sheila Berkeley?" people said. "Ah, yes—the beautiful
one!" Too true, perhaps, for she wore her beauty with a shrug
as if it were an ermine wrap of which she could say, "I suppose
it is lovely, but then I've had it so long!"

Dixon opened his hands and looked at his empty palms. It
was no good temporizing. "Sheila, I can promise nothing," he
said.

For a moment the girl in the blue tweed suit, expertly cut
and altogether immaculate, made no reply. Finally she said, "I

own the greatest racehorses in England—or so I am told. I
employ, in yourself, the best of all possible trainers—or at
least the most expensive. I am fortunate, I know, in having the
paragon of jockeys, not to say that most attractive of men,
your son Kent, to ride for me. And yet . . ."

"And yet," said Dixon, "I cannot promise to win a race—or
predict the outcome. I cannot encourage you to bet the whole
of what you have left on the chance that Templar, great as he
is, will win the Classic. Nor can I swear that he will lose it. A
horse is no machine, no jockey can bring a miracle to pass—
and any trainer who says otherwise is nothing but a lying
fraud!"

He left the desk and strode across the tiny room, a lean man
aged like a leather whip. He turned on her. "Why do you
race?" he asked. "Why—of all people—do you race?"

"For money, Mat." She smiled saying it. "I race for money.
My father didn't, and when he died he was already lost, or
nearly lost through sweet but ruinous sentiment. He loved the
noble horse. I prefer pounds sterling. Does that shock you? I
can't help it. I'm in no position to help it. Templar cost my father ten thousand pounds. One way or another I must get it
back."

"He's earned it ten times over."

She shrugged. "Not for me—and tomorrow we run in the
Classic. It may be rumor, but I've heard that some people make
money on racing—those who know the tricks."

Mat did not yield. "Templar may not win," he said. "He and
Kent will fight to win. They may lose, but they will fight to
win. I can't say more. You can't ask more."

"I do ask more!" She got to her feet and stood before him.
She was not tall, but she was slender, and she was as cleanly
made as any thoroughbred.

Conformation, Dixon thought, but not much else. Breeding, but too small a heart. You saw it everywhere—in men, in horses, and in women.

"I must ask more," she said. Calm had gone out of her voice, and in its place there was an edge of panic, of urgency. "Mat, they're closing in. I'm going to lose it all—the house, the grounds, everything father left—to creditors. Call it my fault. Say I threw the money away, gambled it away It's true, but I don't know how to live without spending. I've got to win on this race, can't you see? It doesn't matter if Templar loses so long as I know how to bet. Fix it for me, Mat, fix it! I don't care how!"

He was coldly quiet. "I care," he said, "and Kent cares. He's not my son and the most respected rider in England for nothing. He will not fix the race, nor will I. Templar will be ridden to win. He will not be held back in order to insure your bet, Sheila. That's what you are hinting, and I tell you it can't be. If you lose—well, then you lose, but you don't quit. Some do, but not, I hope, the daughter of Jeff Berkeley. It wouldn't be . . ."

"Sporting?" she asked. "Is that the word? Shall we be trite, Mat?" She stepped closer to him and met his eyes in open contest. "Look," she said, "you've known me all my life, and you know that I will not submit to living on a pauper's income under the sorrowful eyes of my friends. I will not submit to public disgrace for my debts. If I could sell Templar I would. I would sell him together with all the trumped-up tales and fiction and nonsense about his great heart, his magnificent spirit, and all the rest. But my father's will prevented me from doing that. So I am trapped. And yet not quite!" He watched her upturned, flawless face, and saw that the arrow was coming. "If you can-

not promise what I ask," she said, "I'm still not beaten. Kent
loves me. He always has—and you and I both know it!"

Long ago he had seen Sheila use her charms as a musician
uses notes and strings. She could create many moods in men,
and not the least of these was desire. Kent was a man like other
men—and young—as young as she. As children, the two had
played together, and the boy's loyalty to that friendship, his
admiration of her beauty, had grown with the years. Now he
was great—or close to greatness—in his craft, his art. Not yet
a Fred Archer, but close and coming closer.

Mat Dixon felt a thickness in his throat—a fear—but he
straightened a little, accepting her challenge.

"We promise a clean race—Kent and I—and nothing
more."

She smiled once, with easy certainty. And then abruptly
she was gone. Mat heard her Bentley start and swing away. He
did not have to look through the window to know that she
would find Kent—probably near Templar's stall. Kent was as
honest as spring rain—had always been. But Sheila was as
lovely as spring itself and harder to deny. And yet—to throw
a race, a career and all one's honor away for a girl—for one like
that . . .

"Not my son," Mat Dixon said.

He spat the thought away and went out into the cleansing
air. But he saw the girl's blue Bentley near Templar's stall and
knew there was cause for doubt.

Kent Dixon stood by the stable gate on whose arch was
stenciled the words: "On the Turf, and Under It, All Men Are
Equal." It was hardly profound, and maybe it wasn't true, but
he and his father had always liked to think it was.

He took his thoughts from the legend and looked into the

blue compelling eyes of Sheila Berkeley. He was plainly torn
between conflicting things. His face—an inquiring, forthright face, masking no secrets, was somber now. Unlike most
riders, he was tall—as tall as the great Fred Archer had been.
He was lean, of course, almost as lean as the rails he loved to
ride against. And he was hard. In most things he was hard,
with the thonglike hardness of those who can, with feeling
hands and constant will, direct the unleashed power of a thoroughbred. But was he hard in this?

He swung his glance from the girl to the old and intimate
horizon, then back again to the lavish fortune of her hair.

"Kent, I'm lost," she said, "unless you help." And he listened.

He listened to each word and watched her tears. He held
her close—and this he had not done since childhood days,
vanished days. Not since the incident—the incident they
never spoke of now. Had it not been for that, he thought, he
might have struck her for what she was begging him to do.

But he remembered the long ago day when Sheila had been
trapped in a loose-box by an angry stallion. It was a stallion
the tawny-haired girl had loved with courageous passion—
but not with understanding.

She had loved his smooth and massive beauty, but all the
while there was fear in her, and this she fought because of him,
but she did not know how to keep evenly burning the flame of
his spirit. In those days she thought that love and admiration
were enough, and she offered both. She went boldly one
morning into the stallion's loose-box and closed the door behind her.

It was not a new thing; she had done it before—timidly, at
first, and then with greater ease. But on this morning the stallion was at his feed, and she entered too quietly. Startled, he

turned on her and let his fright blaze into fury. He whirled and tried to reach her with his teeth and with his hooves.

For long and terrifying minutes, she cringed under the feed-box, beating him off with her tiny riding hat, weeping—for fear, and for his faithlessness.

It was Kent who found her, Kent who got her out, and in his boyish arms she had sought comfort for her terror and her childish sorrow.

An incident, he thought, of no importance. And yet it seemed to shut her heart against so many things. It was as if forever afterward she had been afraid to open it lest more hurt enter it. She hated horses now, and from that simple hate worse things had grown—cynicism, hardness. One day something might happen to change all that—one day.

Now she needed him—and more than anything else, he wanted her to need him. It was his chance, and yet he knew that what she asked of him—the whole of his honor, of Templar's honor too, in a way—was a heartbreaking gift to make.

He held her at arm's length and looked at her and shook his head. "You don't know, Sheila, what it means to cheat in a race. Sometimes you read about it. More often you hear rumors, usually untrue. You get to thinking that all riders cheat to win—or to lose. You think it's natural, but it isn't. Not for me."

Tears made stars of her eyes, "I know it, Kent." She was pleading now. "But I appeal to you because I must. I've done wrong things—spent money out of boredom, out of loneliness maybe. I've borrowed it falsely on false promises. I admit that. Now I'm confronted with disgrace, and I can't bear it. I have four days to produce four thousand pounds. And if I fail, I'm leaving England, Kent."

He did not flinch, nor speak, nor make any gesture. But

longing and indecision were suddenly in his eyes. She kissed him full upon the mouth. "I'm betting against Templar," she said. "Don't let me down!" And then she vanished.

Night left its post, and race day came. Mat Dixon's stables, immaculate and gleaming, like the barracks of some proud regiment, were hushed but active. Each of the many stables around the great grandstand was a guarded camp in which some hoped-for Achilles of the turf abided moodily, or some too-eager Hector fidgeted on polished hooves while a thousand husbandmen and handlers counted hours and, throughout the land, ten million Englishmen plotted bets.

Some horses tremble before a race, some ease the tensions of their nerves by spurts of anger, and there are some who brood. But all are conscious of the day—sensible of the approaching trial—wanting it, living toward it. For the thoroughbred who races because he must is not often seen on any track; he cannot win, not even against a poorer horse with a love of running in his heart. Sinew and bone and blood make a horse, but spirit makes a horse race.

Templar was quiet, statue-still. His the great name, his the obligation to be calm. He watched and waited.

A big horse, he dwarfed the grooms. A gleaming horse, his chestnut coat accepted light like amber. Wise in his way, his eyes were large and deeply knowing, and his ears—scarcely longer than the finger of a man—were tilted as if to catch each tick of passing time.

Kent Dixon looked at him and shook his head. "Templar," he said, "this ought to be your race. You want it, and you've got it in you. I have wanted it for years, but now . . ." He did not finish.

With sadness in his hands, he stroked the shoulder of the

stallion. "You can't always win," he said, and, saying it, he turned to see his father in the doorway.

Mat Dixon smiled to see a horse that he had trained within an inch or two of that improbable goal, perfection, to see his son, motherless from birth, conform so closely to what he wanted in a son. These things brought fulfillment near to him. He thought it would be nearer, if now—today—he might see this son, a product of his heart, ride Templar, a product of his skill, to victory in that race all horsemen longed to one day win. But his smile passed swiftly, for the eye of his memory saw another smile challenging his own.

"You're worried, Kent," he said. "It's Sheila."

Kent nodded. His eyes, grey like his father's, were somber now and inward looking. But they held a knowledge.

"It's partly Sheila," he said. "But you mustn't hate her. She can't help having been born to what she was. I love horses; I was born to it. She loves luxury, wastefulness. She was born to that, but one day she will change."

"She was born to selfishness," Mat Dixon said. "She was born with a hollow heart! Forget the girl—until tomorrow. Today we race. Today—"

Kent stopped him. He took his hand from Templar's shoulder. "We may not win," he said. "We may not even place. I have to tell you that." He watched his father's lips tighten now, the muscles of his jaw set hard. He went on, "There's a fault in Templar. You can't see it, but it's there. At times I feel it in my hands during workouts, during races. I've told you that, I tell you now, again."

Mat Dixon fought his rising doubt, his rising anger. Was he being told, being warned in these blunt terms that the girl had won against him—that Templar would be held from probable victory on this trumped-up theory of a hidden fault? Had he trained thoroughbreds for forty years for this? He ran expert eyes over Templar's magnificent body. This horse was perfect, as perfect as a horse could be.

Mat spat into the straw bedding. True, Kent had twice before hinted at some hidden fault in the great stallion—some inherent weakness he seemed to sense but constantly disproved by winning race after race on Templar. Mat Dixon let his anger go in a soundless sigh. There was no better rider in England than his son, but perhaps no more uneven a judge of horses—and of women.

Mat looked at his watch. In a few hours they would be at the post. On fire with this futile love, this futile faith in Sheila, Kent clearly planned to throw the race. Well, a single splinter of time would tell. There would be an instant, Mat knew, an instant of decision when Kent would have to cheat, or not cheat. At the point of that sharp moment, he would have to check Templar—or ride Templar. All plans, all other things aside, it was a question as to whether his son, at the final point, the crucial point, could discard his honor for a lovely face.

He thought not. Surprisingly he smiled. "I trust you, Kent, to do your best. I trust Templar to give his best. He always has; he always will. He's not a quitter—you will not make him one."

He left the stall and went into the sunlight like a man unburdened. His son made a hopeless gesture with his hands and stared at the brooding horse.

By midafternoon the Newmarket grandstand overflowed with people until, from a distance, it was like the mouth of some huge horn of human plenty. The people were tense, the thrill of the impending contest already burning in their blood.

For not time, but struggle, is the essence of a horse race—not stopwatch figures, but rivalry. Who cares how brief the time, how shaved by tenths of seconds, so long as in that time a man's heart may add its tiny drumbeat to the massive music of pounding hooves? Deplore the bets, bewail the gambling, but all of this is not what it seems, for there are people who will bet on a horse for love of him. And, if he loses, they will bet on him again, not caring much, so long as they can see him run. Saint Simon—Seabiscuit—Gallant Fox. What clings to these remembered names is not the smell of gathered money. It is a certain aura that the valiant and the deep of heart leave always in their passing.

Templar was building such a name. His character was such that men too shrewd to do it would bet on him against all comers, at all times, since not to do it seemed a faithless thing.

The crowd was for Templar. And the crowd had voice, a single voice that could swell like the sound of surf, or subside like a waning tide. It could indicate many things—hope, anger, pleasure, sometimes contempt. It could ride the moment. And the moment came.

The paddock opening was cleared, and through this clearing, lined with men whose labor and whose skill was fiber to the sport, the horses filed.

All were great—or so it seemed—all magnificent, or so they looked. No eyes save expert ones could find a fault. But there were such eyes.

The eyes of trainers were sharp, and they were quick. They penetrated style and manner and gleaming coats to see, beneath, a lurking weakness or hidden strength. The trainers bit their pipes, or rubbed their jaws; they watched the horses and pondered on their chances.

But not Mat Dixon. He stood apart, alone among the many, and saw a thing he did not want to see. Templar was last to leave the paddock for the track, and as he left with Kent, resplendent in his gold and purple silks, a glistening head—the head of Sheila—shone as she moved in the swaying crowd.

In a moment she was at the stallion's side, and Mat Dixon saw his son's firm hands draw gently on the reins. He saw Templar pause—nervous now, for the time was near—and he saw, but did not hear, the exchange of words between Kent and the girl. It was short, as casual as a greeting. But it was more. Much more. It was a question and an answer. It was decision.

With it, the girl turned and went, unhesitating, toward the betting booths. Graceful, vivid among the hundreds, she was like a self-assured child walking in a wood.

Kent watched her go, then straightened in the saddle, but he did not seek his father's face. He leaned forward, and he spoke softly to Templar.

The stallion dipped his shapely head and flicked his hooves as if to say that, lacking wings, he could still fly. And then they cantered up the track and took the cheering of the crowd. It swelled and thinned and swelled again, and when it tapered to its final hush, Mat Dixon found his box, his binoculars in hands more tense than they had ever been at any race in forty racing years.

He did not turn toward Sheila's box, and she did not look toward him. Expressionless, unspeaking, they waited for the start.

A struggle, a shout, a soothing voice, horses fighting to be free. The starter's hand poised high; the barriers, inanimate but tense. Such is the prelude to a race.

There is a stillness, a nervous murmur from the crowd, and then again a stillness. The starting gate has every eye; the moment is unbreathing. It dangles like a drop that will not fall. But then it does; a drop of time falling—fallen.

Mat Dixon saw the barrier rise and heard the swift, familiar thunder of the crowd. He saw the human sea surge toward the rail. He heard the cry "They're off!" But he did not add to the cry.

The start was clean with no horse left behind and no horse far enough ahead to be alone. The field of twelve was like a cloud, close-bunched and dark and building speed. It passed the stands where people now were motionless, making no sound, hearing nothing save the velvet drumming on the turf.

Templar was last, restrained by Kent—a band of weightless color bending low. Both horse and rider knew such things as must be known. Both horse and rider knew such things as others knew—or more. They did not press, or fight the field, or flaunt the power that they had. Not yet. Not now.

They did not seek the rail. In one quick move they might, Mat Dixon thought, but now they played the cautious game, and played it well.

The turn was made, the pace increased, and the back stretch spread before the swiftly gliding little storm of crouching men and faster drumming hooves.

A horse called Ariel had the lead—a driving bay with piston stride—hard, rhythmic, and determined. Behind him—just behind—was Chanticleer, running heavily, but fast. This was the one to fear, Mat Dixon knew, the one to watch. He was well ridden, and he never tired. Time and again he had plunged to victory against smoother, fleeter horses through sheer weight of muscle and strength of sinew—through that and heart. Chanticleer had heart. So had Templar—and the two had never met, till now.

Mat Dixon raised his glasses to his eyes and let a smile bend his lips—tentative but full of hope. He swore in silence for his doubt of Kent. The boy was riding.

The boy was riding hard, and now the crowd gave out a stirring growl that rose to thunder, broke to cheers then steadied on the single cry: "Templar!"

For Kent was doing what he did so well. The field—the moving cloud—had thinned as if a wind had scattered it. Twelve horses reached the final turn, but only three were fighting for the lead—black Chanticleer, the bay Ariel, and Templar like rusty gold. The rail, the inside track, was needed now—and Kent was taking it. He had no room: they gave him none, but he was taking it.

Deftly, with unerring hands, he edged Templar so close to the rigid bars that it seemed both horse and rider must crash against them. But they did not crash. They fought their way.

The voice of the crowd rose clear and vibrant. Mat Dixon laughed aloud for pride and threw his laughter toward the cool blonde head of Sheila Berkeley, who did not hear and did not move.

Like a blade, the boy cut Ariel from the race. The turn was made, and the homestretch was a battleground for two— Templar and Chanticleer.

Silence again. The crowd is still. The swallows flying low, swing lower. A throat is cleared, a hat is crushed in nerveless hands. The grandstand creaks.

Desperately, blindly almost, surely with pain in lungs and heart, the two Titans, each with outstretched neck, each with burning, ebbing strength, beat back the time, shame the distance and loom closer length by length.

There is no dust on this green turf, this English turf, the air is clean. The end of a race is clearly seen by any eager eye— at times, too clearly—at such a time as this.

Mat Dixon saw it. Thousands saw it. The cool, unruffled Sheila saw it. Perhaps Chanticleer himself saw Templar suddenly give ground when there was at last no hand's breadth to be spared.

It was a little ground, not much. So little that at first nobody believed it. Could Templar quit? He never had. Could Templar lose? That came to every horse, but this was strange. He seemed at once, to slow his stride—to fight, yet not to fight. He seemed at once to lose his heart, to lose his will—to yield, breath by breath, to Chanticleer, a massive shadow now, blotting the glow of courage that, until this moment, had clung to Templar's name.

Mat Dixon rose and let his glasses dangle on their strap. They had no purpose now. He did not need them to see the end—to see Templar fall back, held surely by a subtle hand—Kent's hand, held so cleverly that the mimicry of courage was almost real as the two great gleaming thoroughbreds bore down fighting (so it seemed) for victory.

Templar was close—a neck behind—and the burden that he carried then was more than man and leather. For the crowd had jeered. The crowd's hosannas had turned to scorn, as wine can turn to vinegar.

And before these jeers, he lost. Before the throng's contempt, he failed—a blood-gold champion, shamed, discredited, not because he did not win, but because in the eyes of those who watched, in the eyes of those who believed in him, he quit.

Night came, inevitable and kind. The grandstand stood deserted, as empty as the half-born moon that shone upon it. The Classic was over; the Classic was won, and the name Chanticleer rolled on the tongue of racing England.

Mat Dixon sat alone. It seemed to him that here in the bar of the Boar's Head Inn, among the scattered voices of unwor-

ried men, he could be more alone than if he sat before the por-
traits on his cottage walls—the champion thoroughbreds, the
silver trophies, the pictures of his son.

He seldom drank, but now he tried and found it bitter in his
throat. It answered nothing, changed nothing. For the tenth
time, he pushed the half-full glass away.

He could not believe what he had seen, but he had seen it.
Behind closed eyes, he still could see it, the greatest horse in
England quitting when a race was nearly won. Being forced to
quit—there was no escape from that, he thought—because
his own son had sold his name, his whole integrity, for a woman's smile and a thatch of shining hair.

Well, her inheritance was safe, her purse was full, her shame
avoided. Certainly she had bet against her own Templar, sure
in the knowledge he would be robbed of his victory. How bra-
zen it now seemed—Kent's effort to convince him of a hidden
weakness in the stallion, when, today, Mat Dixon had watched
his favorite, and the people's favorite, beat the best that England offered—pass them as lightly as a shadow—until the
end.

Until the end. He cupped his hands against his eyes and
tried not to think. He looked at his glass but did not touch it.
He couldn't sit here forever. He would have to face the boy.

He put his hands on the edge of the table and began to rise,
then paused. Kent stood before him, confronted him, blocked
his exit. There was no fear in the boy's face, no repentance.
His eyes were as hard as his father's, and as bitter. They caught
the accusing stare and threw it back.

"Say it," his father said. "Say what you came to say."

Kent stepped back then. He was breathing deeply, and
when he spoke, the movement of his lips was imperceptible.

"The race killed Templar," he said. "He died three hours ago."

Somewhere in the room a stranger was laughing. Somewhere a glass tinkled against another glass. Somewhere a clock marked time. But all of these sounds were silence to Mat Dixon. He rose in silence, hearing nothing, and faced his son with unbelieving eyes.

"I know what's on your mind," Kent said. "I know why you're here. Maybe you had a right to wonder, even to doubt, but you were wrong. We worked to win. I never rode harder. Templar never fought harder. But it's more than that—too much more."

He paused and motioned his father to a chair. Mat Dixon sat in it, waiting.

"Down the homestretch we were winning," Kent said. "You saw it, everybody saw it. We were coming home—and then it happened. The thing I tried to tell you about happened. Templar broke. He went on fighting, but his strength was gone. I felt it leave his body. I felt it running out under my hands and knees. I could do nothing. I couldn't even have slowed him if I had tried. He went on to the end—and lost."

"And died," Mat Dixon said.

Kent stared at the knuckles of his hands. "And died," he said, "two hours later. We brought him back; he tried to eat, but couldn't—and you weren't there.

"I sent for Kimberly and the other vet. It wasn't any good. He was dead when they got there."

Mat Dixon reached for his glass but did not lift it. "You found out why?" Mat Dixon asked. "Thoroughbreds don't die like that. They die, but not like that."

Kent stared at the paneled wall, through it, beyond it. "I did what had to be done," he said. "I had an autopsy. I had to know—and now I know. Listen, Dad." He swung his eyes to the eyes of the older man. "Listen," he said, "for the whole of his life—and for the whole of every race he ran and won, and for those he tried to win—Templar had one lung. Not two like every other horse, but one. He was born that way. We know that now, but he never knew it. He was a racehorse and he had to run, begged to run. That's how he died, that's why he died and why he lost today—breathing hard because he could breathe no other way—fighting, wondering perhaps why each race seemed longer, why every horse seemed stronger than he. But fighting—fighting always, all the way—until he broke, with ten thousand heartless fools calling him a quitter!"

He swung around as if to hide the blur that dimmed his eyes. In an instant he had pushed through the carefree, laughing men and was gone.

For a long time Mat Dixon sat unmoving. Once in the history of English racing a horse had died like that. It was on the records. And now Templar. One lung. Not two like every other horse but one. And still to race, still to fight with every breath too small, each stride a memory of pain. Was there courage in such a horse? Was there heart?

He left the inn and plodded blindly toward his stables in the night. One thing was in his thoughts—one lurking thing. Since Templar lost, then Sheila must have won. It wasn't easy to think of a horse dying for that. It burned in him, and he went to Templar's stall and stood outside it, hoping to forget.

It was empty now. The deep-eyed stallion was gone—the honest one. He turned, then stopped.

The weeping in the empty stall was deep and unashamed— woman's weeping. He took a step, then stopped again; he could not leave. He heard the voice and knew it. He heard the other voice, and it was Kent's. He could not keep himself from glancing through the door.

Moonlight lay like hoarded treasure on the straw. The golden girl crouched in it, kneeling, crying. And Kent was there, as soft-spoken as a man should be when a woman cries.

"He tried to win," he said. "I told you to bet on him—and he tried to win."

"I know it, Kent." She lifted her face and the moonlight caught it. Sorrow had softened it. Tears had gentled it.

"I bet it all," she said, "all on Templar and on you. I couldn't have borne it otherwise. I know that now. I lost everything, and so I am free. I'm free to work—at something, anything. Don't let me be a quitter, Kent."

He smiled and stroked her hair as if she were a child he remembered—a sobbing child frightened by a horse she loved.

"You saw him run," he said, "you saw him break. Templar was half a horse inside—and still he ran. Can we be quitters now?"

aav3649

VERMONT STATE COLLEGES

0 0003 0407790 2

LIBRARY
VT TECHNICAL COLLEGE
RANDOLPH CTR VT 05061

HB 9 T